THE SWAN SUIT

KATHERINE FAWCETT

The SWAN SUIT

Douglas & McIntyre

1 2 3 4 5 — 24 23 22 21 20

Douglas and McIntyre (2013) Ltd.
P.O. Box 219, Madeira Park, BC, V0N 2H0
www.douglas-mcintyre.com

Edited by Silas White
Cover design by Anna Comfort O'Keeffe
Text design by Carleton Wilson
Printed and bound in Canada
Printed on 100 percent recycled paper

Douglas and McIntyre (2013) Ltd. acknowledges the support of the Canada Council for the Arts, the Government of Canada, and the Province of British Columbia through the BC Arts Council.

LIBRARY AND ARCHIVES CANADA CATALOGUING IN PUBLICATION

Title: The swan suit / Katherine Fawcett.
Names: Fawcett, Katherine, 1967- author.
Description: Short stories.
Identifiers: Canadiana (print) 2020015303X | Canadiana (ebook) 20200153048 | ISBN 9781771622608 (softcover) | ISBN 9781771622615 (HTML)
Classification: LCC PS8561.A942 S93 2020 | DDC C813/.6—dc23

For Jack and Lilah

Contents

The Swan Suit

The white swan twisted her neck around and prodded her beak under the feathers on her backside. When she found the zipper head, she gently pulled it along a seam on her spine, up between the base of her wings and up the back of her neck as high as it would go.

The swan's outer layer split apart in an upside-down *V*.

A little wiggle, a stretch and a shrug, and the swan suit crumpled to a heap at the feet of a fair young maiden. She picked up the suit, brushed off the sand and dirt and hung it delicately on a tree branch. Then she rolled her shoulders back, cracked her knuckles, shook out each ankle, walked into the cold lake until she was waist-deep, raised her arms over her head and dove in.

The suit of feathers fluttered in the breeze like the flag of a magical country.

A stocky young fisherman standing on a dock nearby heard the splash that broke the morning's silence. He saw the naked girl frolicking in the deep water on the far side of Mosquito Lake and held his fishing rod perfectly still, not even daring to breathe, so he could watch her without being seen. Never before had the fisherman been in the presence of such beauty. Such perfection.

She leapt playfully forward in a somersault and the fisherman nearly fainted when her buttocks cut through the water's surface, disappeared and were followed by an arc of delicate toes. When she finally burst up for air, mouth open wide and eyes squeezed shut, a bead of drool dangled from the middle of the fisherman's bottom lip.

A rainbow trout nibbled the bait off his fish hook and swam away, scot-free.

After a few minutes, the maiden exited the lake. Drops of water slid down her body like butter melting off a cob of bronzed Chilliwack corn. She twisted her hair to squeeze the moisture out and laid it over one shoulder. Unaware of the fisherman's gaze, she took her swan suit from the tree and stepped back into it, dressing like a burlesque dancer in reverse. She used the serrated edges of her swan beak to carefully close the zipper. Then she shook her tail feathers, stretched her neck, gave a little honk, and after a few powerful beats of her wings, flew away.

Does our fisherman call the Audubon Society of Western Canada and report a new breed of *Cygnus*, one that encapsulates a woman of flesh and blood within its feathery exterior? Or would the *National Enquirer* be more appropriate? *Exposed! Half bird/Half woman Shocks BC Bachelor with Nude Waterplay!* Does he contact his local airstrip or the aviation board? Let them know that someone dressed in a bird costume is flying around the jurisdiction, perhaps presenting a danger to low-flying aircraft? Or does he laugh it off and check for hidden cameras? Maybe someone's playing a prank on him. Maybe the video will show up online and he'll be the butt of jokes for a few days, tweeted and retweeted, and then everyone will forget about it, except for him.

No, our fisherman is a romantic guy. He believes in destiny and falls in love.

"I've found my soulmate," he said to his mother that evening after recounting the day's events. "She's sublime. Beautiful *and* monogamous."

He knew the story sounded absurd, but he told her anyhow. Perhaps she didn't believe him. You couldn't blame her if she didn't; like most fishermen, he'd been known to stretch the truth.

"As the honeybee loves the flower, do I love the swan-woman," he said dreamily. "Of her sweet nectar do I yearn to drink."

"So," said his mother, thrumming her thick fingers on the countertop. "No fish?" It was past suppertime and the fisherman's mother, a woman of considerable weight and appetite, was famished. She went to the kitchen pantry and took out her bow and one arrow.

"Mama, it was love at first sight," he swooned. "With this nymph—this goddess—as my bride, I shall be the envy of all the men in town. Who else could claim their wife has the grace of a swan, the face of an angel and the body of a Victoria's Secret model?"

The fisherman's mother belched inside her throat and blew it out the side of her mouth. She used to be a beauty queen, but that was a long time ago. She didn't believe in soulmates anymore.

"Quiet," she said. "I need to concentrate."

The fisherman's mother was a gifted archer, and her talents had served them well on days when the fish didn't bite. Decades earlier, she'd decided she needed something to fall back on when she lost her looks; when her hair turned grey, when her skin became flaky and when fat and gravity had their way with her torso and breasts. So she took up archery and practised daily. Now, whenever her son failed to bring home fish for dinner, she would wait for a small animal to wander innocently into the garden—usually a rabbit, raccoon or squirrel, but sometimes a woodpecker, once a stray cat and once a three-legged Welsh terrier—point her weapon through a hole in the torn kitchen window screen, draw back her bow and release her arrow with a sharp twang. She never missed. But, like most former beauty queens, she was lazy. Once she'd killed her prey, it was her son's responsibility to go outside, pull the arrow out of the bleeding animal's body, skin it and prepare it for supper.

"Believe it or not, kiddo, I have some experience in the field of courtship and love. So I suggest you pay attention." She shut one eye and took aim from between the green and yellow checkered curtains. "Go to the lake as usual tomorrow morning..."

The point of the arrow was a missile with a direct path into the heart of the hapless creature nosing for a grasshopper at the far side of the potato patch. *Fwonk!* A marmot. Right between his big brown eyes. She placed the bow on the kitchen table, wiped her nose on her sleeve and tucked a few stray hairs back into her bun.

"...with a box of chocolate. High quality, not just any old crap. I don't know much about swan food, but believe you me, no girl can refuse fine chocolate. And don't start talking about babies right off the bat. That'll turn her cold."

They had roasted marmot and fried potatoes for dinner that night. To be honest, the meat wasn't very good. Too tough. If she'd had her way, she would have eaten tender, juicy lamb chops every night. Or lamb shanks. Some kind of kebab. A lamb gyro, wrapped in a pita pocket with cucumber/yogourt sauce and some thinly sliced red onion. But what were the chances of a baby sheep stumbling upon the cottage? Slim to none. No one in the region kept sheep. Too many wolves.

The next day at dawn, the fisherman settled himself on the dock, obscured by a half-fallen tree that leaned across the water, and scoured the lake and shore for a sign of his love. His plan was simple: offer her chocolates, recite a haiku, flex his biceps and before long they'd be exchanging vows.

He cast his line and waited. For almost an hour, there was no sign of any naked girl frolicking. No splashing, bouncing, fleshy maidenhood. He was about to give up when, between some reeds on the far side of the lake, the fisherman spotted an elegant swan gliding along the water, moving its head ever so slightly as it propelled forward, like the hand of a monarch waving to her subjects. Its beak was the colour of marigolds, its body the size and shape of a pillow and its neck curved to form a perfect half heart. The fisherman puffed out his chest as if he were the other half.

From what he could tell, the creature was 100 per cent bird. Could the fair maiden from the day before *really* be disguised as this large waterfowl? The fisherman's brain felt like a tangled knot of fishing line as he considered a suit of feathers containing a woman of flesh. He put a hand to his eyebrow to shade his view and watched the swan intently. It scooped its neck down into the water, presumably to eat a bug.

Impossible, he thought. *That is a swan through and through. Yesterday's wicked sun must have caused my eyes to play me the fool! A cruel jest! My heart, tricked. My dreams, shattered.*

After a short while the swan waddled ashore. It shuffled its webbed feet a few times in the sand, manoeuvred its neck in a way the fisherman thought quite unnatural, and in one smooth motion, its body appeared to split like a bag of grain sliced open by a knife. But instead of kernels pouring out, the golden-haired maiden emerged. The giant wings, the white feathers, the black mask around the eyes and the marigolden beak—all that had been swan—fell to a heap at the girl's bare feet like a feather boa off a showgirl on a Las Vegas stage.

Oh, glorious day! It hadn't been heatstroke *or* hallucination! She really was disguised as a swan, the bird of royalty and passion. No wonder she was so graceful and regal. No wonder he'd fallen in love.

The girl picked up the swan suit, hung it neatly on a tree branch, waded out up to her waist, then dove into the lake, still seemingly unaware of her watcher. *She must be under a spell that turns her into a swan*, thought the fisherman. He knew quite a bit about spells. He'd read his Grimm and his Hans Christian Andersen.

The fisherman imagined walking into the Buzz Cut Tavern for Poetry Slam Open Mic Night with his muscular arm around the girl's slender waist. "Go on, Honey," she'd say, and nudge him playfully with her elbow. "Read the one you wrote for me on our wedding day." He imagined playing Pictionary with her and his mother at the little kitchen table late into the evening; how the two women would laugh together, perhaps even conspire against him in good-hearted fun. Then he imagined the girl in his bed, her body against his, and became light-headed. He placed his palms flat upon his quads until the feeling passed.

Unfortunately, what he couldn't imagine was walking over to her, introducing himself and proposing to her. He, a lowly fisherman. Muscular, yes. Buff, some might say. Handsome enough, with all the right parts in all the right places. A strong Boggle player with a flair for language. All in all, a decent catch. But deep down, the fisherman was awkward and shy. He didn't have much (any) experience with young women. He always felt uncomfortable in his own skin around them.

What if she laughed in his face? What if she screamed and ran—or flew—away? What if she slapped him, like they did in old movies? His feet felt as if they'd become boulders he could not lift. He put a hand deep into his pants pocket and jostled his testicles around, but still he could not muster the courage to approach her.

At his last Toastmasters International meeting, the Table Topics Master had told them courage was only a matter of semantics. *Don't call yourself nervous. Call yourself excited!* The fisherman had been psyching himself up for an extemporaneous public speaking exercise on the topic "When Thirty-Somethings Live with Their Parents: Benefits and Pitfalls." The members that night were a supportive audience, but he still found himself stammering, speaking too quickly and saying "um" and "like" far too much.

The maiden finished her swim. She dried off in the sun for a few moments, then carefully put the swan suit back on, zipped the zipper, shook her swanny head a few times, stretched her wings, gave a little toot and flew away.

My cowardice is a cloak around my heart, he thought. *Its dark shroud could cost me my love.* Then he used his Swiss Army knife to slice open the box of Turtles, and ate all twelve.

"Moron!" said the fisherman's mother when he returned home with no girl, no fish and an empty orange-and-white-striped box. "Tomorrow, you take her a nice bouquet of flowers. Girls are suckers for flowers. And at least you won't go and eat them."

She shot a hedgehog that night, but it was small and the meat was gristly. It required substantial amounts of ketchup to be remotely palatable. *One day, I'll get a really good meal,* thought the fisherman's mother. *A true feast.* She figured at least if there was a wedding celebration, the caterers would pull together a decent menu. She would insist on lamb chops roasted with minced rosemary for the main with a nice dollop of mint chutney on the side (all paid for by the bride's parents, of course; in some ways, the woman was a devoted traditionalist).

The next day, the fisherman walked to the lake with his tackle box and fishing rod in one hand, and a bouquet of flowers in the other. He'd bathed and applied smoothening product to his hair.

It wasn't long after settling himself on the dock that he spotted the swan gliding gracefully across the water on the other side of the lake. After a time, the mighty bird climbed ashore, doffed her swan suit, hung it on a branch and plunged into the lake. Once he gave her the flowers and recited some Kahlil Gibran, it would only be a matter of time until the little cottage was filled with the happy sounds of children's laughter, Lego strewn across the floor and the stone pathway decorated with sidewalk chalk drawings. He did a few squat-thrusts on the dock, something that usually helped boost his confidence and got the blood flowing. At this point, he didn't care if she saw him. In fact, that might have made things easier.

But by the time he finished one set, the girl had already left the water. He stuffed his hands deep into his pants pocket as he watched her put on her swan suit, zip it up, nibble a bit of pond scum off her belly feathers, bob her head up and down, extend her wings and fly away.

Aaaarrgh! My hope for love fades like a suntan in October, thought the fisherman, and he flung the bouquet into the lake. Three rainbow trout circled it as it drifted to the bottom, snapping at the raffia ribbon the whole way.

"Idiot!" said the fisherman's mother that night, taking her bow and an arrow from the kitchen pantry in a huff. "So now you've wasted a nine-dollar box of chocolate and a dozen perfectly good carnations. You can't do anything right, can you? How will you ever get a wife? And to top it all off: no fish for three days!"

Fwonk! She shot the first animal she saw.

"Oh joy," she said. "Crow, again."

The fisherman looked at his feet.

"You're too wimpy. No spine. That's your problem."

"Perhaps I could woo her with music," he suggested, brightening at the thought. "It's the language of the heart. I'll bring my mandolin to the lake tomorrow."

The mother remembered his mandolin lessons. "Don't," she said.

"Well, maybe I could ply her with fine wine and ale. Spirits to free her of her inhibitions; release her from the bonds of propriety."

"Bad idea. You don't want a boozer for a wife."

The fisherman's mother knew her boy was no Prince Charming. Sure, he spoke in fancy words, and was strong enough to lift anything that wasn't nailed down or rooted to the earth, but the smell of dead fish was ever-present on his hands and clothes. His face was scarred with pits from a serious case of chicken pox when he was nine. His nose featured a prominent lump at the bridge and nostrils that were not quite level with one another. Their cottage was basically a dinky hovel: low ceilings, hardly any storage space and mould along the bottoms of the window panes.

But he was her only son. He cared for her as she grew old. He was a good boy. Why shouldn't he enjoy some of the pleasures a woman's body can provide a man? Most nights she heard the lonely *squeak squeak squeak* coming from his bed frame after the sun went down. And also in the early hours of the day. And sometimes just after supper. He was healthy and virile. It was only natural that he take a wife. And if this half-woman, half-bird creature was his only hope—and *her* only hope for a daughter-in-law, and for the grandchildren that such a union was sure to produce—then so be it. She hoped that swan-ism was a recessive gene, but she swore she'd love and accept them even if they did come out part bird.

"I have an idea," she said. She bade her boy come closer and whispered something into his ear.

The fisherman's eyebrows lifted and his jaw dropped. "That's cruel," he said. "Do you think it will work?"

The mother smiled. They both knew it would.

"Give that back, right now!" cried the maiden when she emerged from the lake the next day.

The feathery costume was draped over the fisherman's forearm like a cloth napkin on the arm of a server in a fine restaurant.

"Marry me and I will," he said, with the bubbly confidence of someone whose mother has bestowed complete faith upon him. The Table Topics Master would have been impressed too.

"Never!" she cried and tried to grab the garment by its black webbed foot. The fisherman held it over his head, just out of her reach. He had never been this close to a naked woman before. Surprisingly, he did not lose his cool.

"Join me in holy matrimony and you'll get it back, plus so much more."

"Not in a million years."

"With the power of my love and the magic of our earthly desire, I'll release you from your spell."

"Spell? What the hell are you talking about? Give it back!"

"I'll make you the happiest girl on earth. I have a home—indeed, a small castle—in the sunny south forest clearing. We shall dine on fresh fish every day. I have a field full of exquisite root vegetables, and a mother who is a champion marksman and a former beauty queen. I possess the strength of an ox and the wealth of a king and I shall treasure you like the rarest jewel." He took a deep breath so she could know the width of his pecs through his woven shirt.

The girl narrowed her hazel eyes, widened her dainty nostrils and pulled her lips in. "You'll be sorry," she snarled.

"Please, take your time deciding," said the fisherman, who was on a roll. "My love for you is patient. It knows no end." He flung the swan suit over his shoulder and whistled as he walked home.

The fisherman's mother had taken down a fat squirrel with her arrow that evening, and the fisherman skinned it. "I think it went pretty well," he said as he flipped the meat in the frying pan. "I have a feeling we'll be setting another dinner plate at the table in no time." The woman took pride in her son's cocky new attitude. *That's what happens when a man takes the bull by the horns*, she thought. They picked the squirrel bones clean and played Jenga. The fisherman won every game. His mother said she'd had too much coffee that day and her hand was unsteady. The truth was, she was a little apprehensive about the whole daughter-in-law thing. Although it had been her idea, she wasn't so sure about having another woman in her house.

What if she did things differently? Loaded the dishwasher with mugs on the bottom? Forgot to put a sheet of Bounce in the dryer? What if she was a vegetarian?

The next morning the fisherman went to the lake as usual. There was no sign of his future life mate, but he tried to remain optimistic. He cast his line into the water and caught a silver bass, which he took home, fried up and ate with his mother.

"Don't worry," said the old woman, who knew her son had a delicate sense of self-esteem. "She'll come around." They played Chinese checkers until she accidentally knocked the board and sent the marbles rolling all over the floor. She wondered about the girl's housekeeping. She'd heard some horror stories about daughters-in-law. *What if she was a slob? Or worse, a neat freak?*

Night turned to day and again he went to the lake. Again, one fish and no girl.

"Ladies these days are in no rush to settle down and get married," said the fisherman's mother as her son set up for Old Maid. He pulled three of the Queens from the deck and divided the remaining forty-nine cards between them. "Girls like to think they can do and be whatever their little hearts desire: fly off to Timbuktu; become graphic artists or chemists or swans; cut their hair different lengths on either side of their head. Some I hear even turn into boys. Maybe it's just not meant to be." She picked up her cards and began discarding pairs. She scratched her head and a whirlwind of dandruff fell onto the linoleum.

As they pulled cards from each other's hands, made pairs and tried to avoid getting stuck with the dreaded Old Maid, the fisherman's mother thought back to her younger days. She never did feel entirely comfortable as a beauty queen, with her shadow-casting cheekbones, attentive tits, delicate ankles and flat little belly on display at car dealerships on Saturdays and community picnics on Sundays and town parades on holidays. There was a disconnect between her svelte young body and her tough, independent inner self.

Men worshipped her, but they never challenged her to a game of Othello or crib. They asked for her hand in marriage, but never her opinion. They touched her all over her skin, but never penetrated her heart and engaged her mind. As she got older, her body changed. She knew it was inevitable. You look in the mirror one day and don't even recognize your own reflection. You have a different outline and a different appetite; you leave a different footprint. Deep down, you're still the same, but there's something new about the shape of space you take up in the world.

On the third day, the fisherman stood on the dock and wondered whether he'd done the right thing. He feared he might never see the girl again. Perhaps he would never have a wife on his arm and his mother would never become a grandmother.

He cast out his line, caught a small brown trout and went home earlier than usual. If he'd had a tail, it would have been between his legs.

His mother tried to contain her relief by giving advice. "I hate to say it, Son, but if she hasn't come around by now, it's probably game over. Life is short and you don't want to wait around forever. Maybe it's time to start thinking of other opportunities. How about one of the gals in your little talking club?

"Don't say that, Mama. I'm not giving up hope."

He wasn't interested in women from Toastmasters International, or the gym or those who hung out at the Buzz Cut. He was in love with the girl from the lake.

"Settlers of Catan?" asked the fisherman's mother after supper. He told her he didn't want to think that hard.

"Okay then. Monopoly?"

Took too long.

"Fish?"

"Ha ha." He hated that game, and she knew it.

"Well, if you're going to be a stick-in-the-mud, you can be one by yourself." She kissed her son on the forehead and went to get ready for bed.

The fisherman was piling plates on the counter when he noticed a silhouette right outside the kitchen window. He gasped, and scrambled to flick on the porch light. It was the girl. He had no idea how long she'd been standing there watching, but he suspected from her squinty expression, folded arms and the way she was shivering that it had been quite some time.

He opened the window. She stood upon a decorative rock in the garden, still naked, skin marked with dirt and scratches, hair tangled with grass and leaves. Her armpits were hairier than he'd remembered and despite the darkness, he could tell her pubic area had also suffered from neglect. The odour of onions and old mushrooms emanated from her, and the overhead porch light illuminated a fair amount of cellulite on her thighs. Even her breasts looked tired and dirty—not perky and white like they had when she'd first stepped out of the lake. There was so much dirt under her fingernails it was as if she'd been digging for grubs with her bare hands, and there was an ugly scrape on her elbow. For a moment he wondered if the girl was wife material at all. It was obvious she was no winning Bachelorette; no Real Housewife of anywhere. But there was something about her chapped lips that made him want to press his mouth against them. Her greasy hair and bad breath and the dirty scrape on her elbow made her seem somehow more real. More human.

"You win," she blurted through a clenched jaw. "I will marry you."

"P-p-pardon?"

"I said, I accept your proposal."

"You do?"

"But first, give back what you stole."

The fisherman took a moment to consider. "I can't. Not right now."

"Why not?"

"Well, because it's hanging up in the bathroom."

"And?"

"And my mother is in there getting ready for bed. She has a routine. She'll be at least forty-five minutes."

"So what! Go bang on the door. Get her to pass it out to you."

"I can't do that. You don't know my mother. She'd never open the bathroom door for me. We're not that kind of family."

The girl cussed under her breath, something that delighted the fisherman perversely.

"Perhaps you'd like to come inside and wait until she's done. I could make us some tea. Get you a bathrobe and some slippers. We have so much to talk about." He realized as he spoke that the house hadn't been properly tidied up for several months. Dishes were stacked on the counter and table and the compost bucket was overflowing with bones and fur. But, just as her flaws had enhanced his desire for the girl, perhaps an imperfect home would endear him to her.

The girl rubbed her temples. "No. We have nothing to talk about. Just meet me at the lake tomorrow at noon."

"I shall be there," said the fisherman, one hand on his heart. He turned and yelled down the hall, "Mama! Hey Mama!" He wanted to share the joyful news, but she was running the tub and couldn't hear a thing over the water.

The girl stomped one foot impatiently. "Just don't forget what you owe me. And it better be in perfect shape."

Truth was, he was a little worried that the petite swan suit might be a bit stretched out of shape. He suspected that his mother, an XXL, had tried it on while he was out fishing, but he had not confronted her, as it would have caused embarrassment all round.

"Of course. Uh, I mean, of course not. I mean, yes! I'll bring it. It'll be perfect." He was aware that he would have had at least eight points deducted if this were an official Toastmasters presentation, for all the stammering. Maybe he should communicate non-verbally. He reached out to touch her cheek with his finger, but snatched it back when she tried to bite him.

The next morning, the fisherman awoke early. He told his mother all about the girl's nighttime visit.

"Well, I suppose you're gonna have to make it official," she said. "Go fetch my jewellery box."

The fisherman dashed into his mother's bedroom and brought out a small wooden box. She opened it and pulled out the gold ring the fisherman's father had given her when they'd exchanged vows. She'd stopped wearing it years ago, when it had become too tight around her finger. "She might have to get it sized."

"Oh, Mama, thank you so much! You have no idea how much this means to me. Are you sure?"

"Try not to drop it along the way."

The fisherman hugged his mother, who turned away so her son wouldn't see the tear in her eye. He promised he'd be careful and tucked the ring in the front inner pocket of his overalls.

"As the worm becomes the butterfly, today I shall become a man," he said, then blew his mother a kiss.

"Caterpillar, you dolt." But he'd already closed the cottage door and started down the path.

The fisherman arrived nearly four hours before the appointed time, with the swan suit tucked under his arm.

He'd spritzed it with water and thrown it in the dryer for twenty minutes to freshen it up and shrink it back to size. His mother had shown him how to properly fold it. "Don't want this new lady to think you were raised by a pack of wolves," she'd told him, although she complained the thing was more complicated to fold than a fitted sheet.

He placed the white costume beside him on a log near where he'd first seen the girl, and smoothed down the feathers. Not that it mattered; spell or no spell, the fisherman figured she wouldn't be doing bird things once they were wed. As part of the sandwich generation, she would have to balance the demands of caring for an aging mother-in-law with raising young children. Add to that tending the potato patch, keeping house, reading his poetry, listening to him prepare orations and spotting him at the gym. When would she even have the time to fly around?

The sun was near its highest point when the maiden approached, on a path he'd not noticed before. She was still pretty ratty looking. *But of course she was. Where had she spent the night? How did she stay warm?* It dawned on him that he knew very little about her. *Did she have a family? How old was she? Where did she live?* When she was a swan, he assumed she simply flew around, glided on lakes and slept in a big nest of twigs or amongst bulrushes.

"Good day, uh..." said the fisherman, realizing he did not even know her name, "...my darling."

Their eyes met, though she stood a good distance from him.

"You look as luminescent as the full moon on a mid-winter night," he said. Obviously it wasn't true, but he felt the urge to fill the silence. And what woman could resist a carefully placed compliment?

She said nothing.

Slowly, the fisherman stepped forward as if to do a lunge and set one knee upon the ground. He reached into his front inner pocket and pulled out the ring. "With this golden symbol of eternal life, I pledge to you my heart and my name."

The girl stepped forward gingerly, her left arm extended. He was ready to delicately take her dainty—albeit unwashed—hand in his and place the ring upon her finger. It would be the first time their skin had touched. He expected electricity and clenched his buttocks.

But instead of offering her hand, the girl abruptly snatched the ring from the fisherman, who lost his balance and fell to the ground. She examined it in her palm, frowned, then held it between two fingers in the air in front of her where they could both see it, opened her mouth wide, placed it gently upon her tongue and closed her lips. The fisherman leapt to his feet. He was stunned. Was she going to swallow it? That ring had been in the fisherman's family for generations! It was eight-carat gold! Was she out of her mind?

He was about to grab her by the throat and shake the ring out of her mouth when the girl lifted her right hand over her head as if to pull an arrow from a quiver on her back.

She seemed to fumble with something at the top of her skull. Then she drew her hand slowly downward, around the curve on the back of her head, down the neck, along her upper spine. When her arm could reach no farther, the other arm twisted behind from underneath. She continued to pull downward until her fair maiden suit came completely unzipped and fell away on both sides. The fisherman watched in horror as a mangy grey and black creature emerged from within the skin of his betrothed.

For a moment, the thing stood on its hind legs. Its chest was twice the size of the fisherman's. Then it lowered itself to all fours and sniffed the fair maiden suit, a pile of skin and hair and lady-bits that lay crumpled on the ground.

The beast might have been an enormous wild dog, but its head and paws were bigger, its snout longer and its ears more pointed than any dog the fisherman had ever seen. The she-wolf lifted her head and curled back her lips to expose blood-red gums and teeth like nails of jagged pearl.

The fisherman held his breath as the wolf turned her attention away from him and gently picked up the limp fair maiden suit with her teeth. She carried it tenderly, like she would a newborn pup, hung it on a low tree branch and licked the torn spot on its elbow. The fisherman took a slow, careful step backwards. If he could make it to the cottage now, he would be safe. A twig crunched under his foot. The wolf's head spun toward him.

For a moment the fisherman thought if he remained perfectly still, his outfit of earth tones and khaki would camouflage him. The wolf's ears were cocked high and her fierce amber eyes locked on the fisherman's, which were as round and scared as those of a caught fish. She began to move her jaw around as if chewing something, or trying to get a bit of food unstuck from her teeth. The fisherman wondered if she had perhaps torn a piece of flesh off the fair maiden suit. His breath came in jittery puffs through his crooked nose. Then the wolf pulled her lips back again and the fisherman spotted the gold ring, sparkling in the sunlight, dangling from a bottom fang. She lowered her head to the ground, fiddled with something, and a few moments later the fisherman's family heirloom was around a claw on the wolf's left paw.

The empty, fleshy fair maiden suit dangled from the tree behind the wolf, waving like laundry drying, its unfilled breasts hanging like socks, its hair blowing like wheat in a field. The fisherman held his hands upon his belly. His mouth filled with stomach acid and he thought for sure he was going to be sick.

The wolf swaggered toward him on all fours, shoulder blades rising and lowering on her back with each stride. Saliva swung like chains from her mouth and her hackles were raised. There was a heavy smell of wet fur and old meat.

A tiny squeak was all that emerged from the fisherman's throat when he tried to speak. His chin quivered and he could feel his heart beating like fists pounding upon a door.

The wolf came within inches of the fisherman and stood up on her hind legs. She placed her massive front paws on the fisherman's shoulders. A passerby might have thought they were waltzing. The fisherman felt dizzy with fear and confusion. He searched the animal's fiery eyes for any sign of the fair maiden. Or the graceful swan. But all he saw was wolf.

The skin between his legs became warm as he passed water.

Then, the wolf reached a paw around the back of the fisherman's skull, as if to pull him toward her for a kiss. When they were almost nose to snout, she reached under his hair and after a bit of feeling around, hooked her claw—the one wearing the gold band—into a zipper head. With a firm tug, the wolf pulled the toggle down, down, down. It moved smoothly, as if the zipper had been freshly oiled, and the fisherman suit split apart easily along a stretch of seam.

When it was fully opened, the wolf unhooked her claw from the zipper head and the fisherman suit lay in a careless heap on the ground. In the man's place was a small, woolly lamb with squishy pink ears, knobby knees and wide-set eyes. The wolf sniffed, then prodded the meek little creature with its snout. The lamb blinked its white-lashed eyes twice, bleated stupidly, kicked its hooves free of the fisherman suit, and ran as fast as its wobbly legs could carry it into the forest, toward the cottage in the sunny south forest clearing.

The wolf picked up the fisherman suit—not nearly as tenderly as the fair maiden suit she'd picked up earlier—shook off the sand and hung it on a tree branch. It smelled of urine and aftershave and trout.

So. What happens next?

Does our wolf put on the white swan suit that had been stolen from her and fly up above the treetops, silently supported by the wind? Glide across lakes and ponds looking for beetles and snails to eat, and places to nest, her body a symbol of love, faith and mythology?

Or does she put on the fair maiden suit that had brought her such unwanted attention, yet such joy? She yearns to feel once again the sensuality of water upon flesh, the ancient pleasure of skinny dipping, but is she willing to risk being so vulnerable, so exposed?

Perhaps she will roam the woods as a wolf, frightening both humans and animals with her piercing eyes, broad shoulders and evil snarl. She could find a pack and howl with a wolf choir in carnal ecstasy when the moon is full. She might find pleasure in the hunt.

Or maybe she will put on the smelly fisherman suit. Explore what it feels like to wear the body of a strapping young man. She's never been a man before. She might enjoy it. She's always wondered what it would feel like to speak in a deep voice. To grow a beard. To have a penis, big muscles and a doting mother.

She is an adventurous soul.

Why not? she thinks. She knows nothing lasts forever. Skin, fur and feathers are simply costumes, like the cloak of snow the earth wears all winter or the pink accessories the cherry tree dons in the spring. Besides, a game of cards with someone who loves her sure would be a nice way to spend an evening.

She yanks the fisherman suit off the branch, but before she puts it on she uses her teeth to take the gold ring off her claw and spits it, with a powerful hork, into the lake. Three rainbow trout follow it as it sinks, spinning, to the sandy bottom.

The wolf pulls the fisherman suit up over her haunches and tail, tucks in the thick, coarse back fur and the thin, soft, white hair on her belly, and zips it shut. Her new fingers are stubby and clumsy, but she is careful not to snag anything, flesh or fur, as the metal teeth come together.

Then she—now a he—gazes across the water. A fish jumps. If only he had his fishing rod and tackle box. But tomorrow is another day, and he's certain to catch a wonderful fish.

He whistles as he heads up the forest path toward a cottage in the sunny south forest clearing. Inside is a former beauty queen whose zipper pull has completely grown over with old skin and coarse, white hair, leaving only a small bump on the back of her head. Most of the time she doesn't even remember it's there anymore. She's preparing a special marinade of olive oil, oregano, thyme, lemon and rosemary. She chops the herbs as she waits for her beloved son to return and pull the arrow from the woolly body of the animal she's just shot, an animal whose tender, juicy meat she's been craving for so long.

The Devil and Miss Nora

On Tuesday just before noon, the Devil appeared at Li'l Sprouts Daycare Centre.

"Give me one of your children," he said to Miss Nora. "Either you choose which one, or I will." He was dressed in black slacks and a wrinkly black dress shirt. He was carrying a waterproof black bag. His hair was puffier than you'd think for the Prince of Darkness, and not what you'd call jet black. Really, it was dark brown. His teeth were crooked and his skin was pale. If you didn't know his true identity, you might have thought he was just unhealthy. The kind of guy who didn't spend much time outdoors, who played too many video games.

Most of the children were at plastic picnic tables gluing dry noodles onto toilet paper rolls. Some were pushing toy cars along a road map carpet. A few were climbing up and sliding down a staticky plastic slide.

None of the kids saw the Devil. Or if they did, they didn't care. He didn't look like anybody special.

Miss Nora was scooping mac and cheese into red and blue and yellow plastic lunch bowls. She figured the visitor must be the guy doing the new Li'l Sprouts website. He was probably looking for a child to photograph. Still, she had to follow protocol.

"Hi there! Sorry, but have you registered at the front desk?" she asked, wiping her hands on a tea towel.

The Devil had not.

"Off you go then," Miss Nora said. When she reached up to point the way, her blouse lifted slightly at the waist and the Devil noticed part of a tattoo poking out from above her jean skirt. There were two points reaching to the left and to the right of her hipbone, like the ears of a black cat. Or could it be an inverted pentagram? The symbol of Lucifer and the denial of heaven?

"Third hallway on the left."

As he backed out the door, the Devil held down his middle and ring finger with his thumb, lifted the other digits and gave Miss Nora a discreet corna. He knew his task was going to be easy when she responded with a cute little devil's horn of her own, waving all her fingers, but making sure the pinky and pointer stayed high.

Really, the taking of a child's soul was not the Devil's job. He had underlings to do this kind of legwork. But the Demons of Hell had been complaining that with all the overprotective parents these days, it was "so hard" to take possession of a minor's soul. They said it was "brutal" getting a child alone to go through the procedure, with parents always hovering. The Devil wanted to prove that acquisition was doable, that sometimes one must use some initiative to achieve one's goals. Be bold and creative. Or like today, just find a kindred spirit. *But, no. This generation of demons expects everything to be handed to them on a silver platter*, thought the Devil. *So damn entitled.*

On his way to the front desk of the community centre, he passed the gym, a few meeting rooms, a dance studio, a cafeteria, a social services office and a seniors' lounge. In the seniors' lounge, some old people were playing cribbage. Others were watching television or looking at a laptop computer. A few were dozing in comfortable chairs. A man who must have been at least ninety looked up from the card game and caught the Devil's eye. There was a sudden flash of recognition on the old man's pinched, dehydrated face. The Devil held his equipment bag close, tucked his chin down and kept walking.

"Hey you! Wait!" said the man. "Over here!" The Devil saw a cane waving out of the corner of his eye. Desperate people always recognized him and his demons, but the Devil had a rule against negotiating with anyone over sixty-eight. It was kind of a point of pride.

He took a few wrong turns, but eventually managed to find the front desk, registered with the receptionist and headed back through the labyrinthine public facility. This time, the old geezer and a few of his friends croaked at him and waved furiously. A woman lurched forward, looking wobbly without her walker. But our man from the pits of Hell ignored them and picked up the pace.

He arrived back at Li'l Sprouts a bit out of breath. The children were just finishing up their lunch. "Give me one of your... your..." He stopped and put his hands on his thighs.

"Do you want something to drink?" asked Miss Nora.

Before he could answer, she passed him a little cup with giraffes on it. He gulped down the apple juice and felt much better. "*Merci beaucoup.*"

"Ooooh, he speaks in tongues."

The Devil squint-smiled. This was going to be as easy as negotiating a deal with an intermediate-level guitar player.

"So, would you like to choose the child, or shall I?"

Miss Nora took the empty cup from him and said, "You may as well choose. You're the professional." Her mouth curved into an inverted half moon, and dimples appeared under her cheeks. "But first, you'll need to show me your access pass."

"My *what?*"

Miss Nora told him that she didn't want to be rude, but without an access pass, how was she supposed to know that he'd properly signed in?

"It's policy. Now off you go," she said, playfully tugging the ring on her lip.

Again, the Devil passed the gym, the dance studio, the cafeteria, the social services office and the seniors' lounge on his way to the front desk. This time, the grey-hairs were waiting for him. They shouted like a herd of crazed teenagers at a rock concert. The Devil knew they all wanted deals. It was pathetic how little people of this age were willing to give up their souls for: a new pair of eyes to see their great-grandchildren with; a chance to apologize to an adult son or daughter who wasn't speaking to them; one night with George Clooney or Sandra Bullock.

But elder-souls were generally worn out and full of holes. A life of compromises, quashed dreams, regrets and broken promises did that. Again, the Devil hugged his bag close and didn't look their way when he passed their lounge.

The receptionist said, "Silly me!" and gave the Devil a laminated access pass. It said *Guest* on the front and his name on the back in erasable pen. It hung from a lanyard. The receptionist told him to bend down, and she looped it around his neck. While his head was forward, he was thankful he'd let his hair grow out a bit—it completely covered both horns.

The access pass swung to and fro as he walked out the main entrance of the community centre, through the parking lot, around the building and back inside through a side entrance. This way was longer, but he avoided the old people altogether.

Miss Nora met the Devil at the Li'l Sprouts door. He held up the access pass so she could inspect it. She flipped it over. "'Stan.' Gee, that's such a nice old-fashioned name," she said in a quiet voice. She seemed so pleased he thought she might give him a gold star.

He smoothed out the front of his shirt and said, "I'm kind of an old-fashioned guy." The Devil hadn't flirted in a long time. It felt as though ashes were being blown off his heart by a spring breeze. It made him shiver.

But he couldn't forget why he was there. "Okay now, how about one of those little monsters?"

Miss Nora wrinkled up her nose and said, "Actually, it's after-lunch nap time now. So if you could just come back at like 2:15, that would be best." She motioned for him to look over the half wall at the Dream Zone and whispered, "Aren't they just sooooo angelic?"

"Yes. You could say that again," he said, but hoped she wouldn't, as the mention of heavenly spirits caused an involuntary twitch of his right eyelid. He pressed two fingers on his eye to calm the tremor. Then she pointed to a sign that said *Nap Time Is Hush-Hush Time* and shrugged her shoulders as if to say, *Oh well! What can you do?* It was 1:05.

The Devil did the math. He really didn't want to just kill time until 2:15. This had already taken longer than expected, with all that traipsing through and around the building. Those lazy demons back home would be expecting him. He wove his fingers around the lanyard. If he really wanted to get back with *something*, he could always gulp down his pride and go to the seniors' lounge.

But the thing with the very young was that they didn't have regrets or bucket lists or the desire to change themselves. And any desires they did have were realistic and simple enough that they didn't need to sell their souls for them to be fulfilled. If a child simply cried a bit, waited, maybe cried a bit more, someone was bound to feed them, change their diaper, pick them up or hand them a toy. Boom! The deepest wish of his or her puny life, granted. That was what made the souls of babies and toddlers such hot commodities in the underworld. A soul that didn't covet anything was the most valuable thing of all. It was pure potential.

The Devil knew he had to select a fresh kid, take it somewhere private to steal its soul, then return the possessed toddler's physical body, now an instrument of Satan, to Li'l Sprouts before pickup time.

Of course, "stealing a soul" is just a figure of speech. The Devil—or one of the Devil's agents, when they aren't slacking off—doesn't actually *take* a soul anywhere when he (or she) steals it. Rather, the soul stays in the subject's body, but the subject loses control over it and it becomes occupied by dark forces, to forever be a puppet of evil.

"Hello? Yoo-hoo! Earth to Sta-aan!" Miss Nora was waving her hand in front of the Devil's face. "You okay?"

"Sorry. Zoned out. It's just—I'm on a bit of a timeline." He noticed her fingernails, chewed short and painted black.

"All right, fine," whispered Miss Nora. "I'm a pushover." She tucked her hair behind an ear. "You sure you just want one?"

The Devil paused. This woman really thought outside the box. He scratched his chin. He *could* take two. A double whammy.

But, no. Best not to get greedy. During the procurement process, he really needed to focus on a single soul at a time. Besides, he could always come back for seconds.

"One's good."

"Okay then. One it is. Just don't walk on my carpet with your outdoor shoes on."

"Yes ma'am." He took off his loafers and put them in one of the top cubbies. Then he tilted his head down and sniffed around his armpit area discreetly to make sure he didn't smell sulphury.

He walked past the train table and the sandcastle station and the puppet theatre with its basket of felted farm animal puppets and the goldfish bowl on the side counter with a handwritten sign that said *Swimmy the Fish*. All the children were sleeping, some wrapped in fuzzy blankets, some with stuffed animals, some with pacifiers in their mouths. The Devil was looking at the napping kids, figuring out which one's innocent soul he would possess with the immortal and infinite power of almighty evil, when he stepped on a piece of Lego. "Motherfucker!" he mouthed, and bit his own lip to stop himself from screaming. A puff of smoke came out of his nose.

Miss Nora, watching from beside the sink, grimaced. *Oooooouch*, she mouthed. *Poor you!* The Devil kind of laughed, partly because he was embarrassed and partly because it was ridiculous that a piece of Lego could hurt so much. He was also touched, because no one had ever felt sorry for him before, and he had a habit of laughing when he didn't know what else to do or say.

Miss Nora came over, took him by the hand and sat him down on a beanbag chair.

"May I?" she asked, as she plunked down on the ground in front of him and tugged gently on the toe of his black sock.

He yanked his foot back.

"Don't be shy," she said. "I have a magic touch."

He grimaced and pinched his nose.

"Oh, you!" Miss Nora waved off his modesty. "No need to worry; I've dealt with worse stinks than this!"

"You are one brave soul," said the Devil.

She rolled his sock off and gave his foot a little rub. There was a thin cleft along the length of his arch, from the middle toe to just before his heel. If there was sock lint in it, she either didn't notice or was too polite to mention it.

"Better?" she said softly.

She had some kind of oil on her hands. The smell was intoxicating.

He nodded.

"This is a blend of pure essential oils of frankincense, lavender and cypress, which all have proven anti-inflammatory and analgesic properties. It'll help ease the pain."

"Mmmmm. Yes."

She kept rubbing. Went up his ankle a bit. "I should give you something for your dry skin too," she said. "No offence intended."

"None taken. It *is* an issue for me."

"You'd like helichrysum essential oil. It really helps restore fluids."

"You had me at helichrysum."

"Remind me before you leave. Free sample."

"That'd be sweet."

She smiled and they looked at each other for an extra few seconds. It felt like a scene in a movie. His foot still rested on her lap and he completely forgot where he was, who he was.

"Well then," she said, breaking the spell, "which one do you want?" She looked across the sea of dozing tots.

The Devil is suspicious by nature, and despite Miss Nora's co-operation, a voice inside his head told him it was strange that she didn't put up a fight at all for the children. And technically, he needed confirmation of permission to access the child's eternal soul. Otherwise, the deal would be invalid. She was, for all intents and purposes, the children's official, legal guardian while they were under her care.

"You *do* know why I'm here, right?" whispered the Devil as he put his sock back on.

"Heck, yes. Of course I do, Stan! And I hope that with your work, a far greater number of families will be reached. Children are the future. We need to care for their little souls. I know that with your special skills you'll be able to capture the essence and spirit of childhood just right."

He felt like a dog who'd just been patted on the head.

"I have a drawer full of permission slips and waivers, if you need. They're all part of the enrolment package. I could make copies?"

"That's okay, I just wanted to make sure we were both on the same page."

"Same page, same chapter, same book. And Stan? I'm super sorry about putting you through the wringer earlier, with the access pass thing."

"No worries. We all have a job to do. You do yours well."

She leaned toward him and looked from side to side as if there might be a burglar around. "Thanks. These days you can't be too careful."

"Amen," said the Devil, and gave her a wink.

He couldn't remember the last time he'd felt so comfortable with another being, living or dead, possessed or free-spirited. He felt he could finally just relax and be himself.

"You are going to use a flash, right?" she said.

"Yes," he said. "A flash. There's usually a flash."

The Devil chose a girl with short, curly blond hair on a mat beside the *Francophone, C'est Fantastique!* bookshelf. She was cuddling a pink stuffed goat. He leaned down to pick her up.

Miss Nora put her hands on her hips and shook her head. "Oh, no, no, no, no, no. Don't take Lilah," she said. "She's got a lazy eye."

The Devil didn't want to argue, so he tucked the girl's blanket under her chin and pointed to a boy two mats over. He was dressed in a Spider-Man costume, even though it was nowhere near Halloween.

"Bad idea," said Miss Nora. She put her hand on his bicep and gave it a little squeeze. "That's Jack. Cute, but he's ADHD. You'll have a hard time getting him to sit still."

It felt as if there was an electric current pulsing through his arm, right under the place where her hand was touching him.

"Hey, do you want to go multicultural?" she asked, pointing across the room. "That's Charlie. He's from the Philippines. He's sooooo adorable."

In truth, he didn't care which one he took. Lazy eye, ADHD, Caucasian, Parisienne, Martian. Normally he would have just grabbed the closest kid and bolted. But being next to Miss Nora—having her whisper to him, touch him, laugh with him—it felt exquisite. Stepping over the mats with her felt as if they were traversing an alpine meadow, so careful not to step on the precious flowers.

"How about this little fella?" said the Devil, using his foot to tap the mat of a pale boy in green overalls. He was curled up like a fortune cookie and had his thumb in his mouth.

Miss Nora took a long step over two children sleeping side by side. Her skirt crept up her legs and the Devil felt woozy when he saw the soft geometry of her tanned knees. She stumbled and windmilled her arms to catch her balance. He reached out his hand to steady her.

"Whoa, thanks," she said, and looked so deeply into his eyes he was sure she'd be able to see the flame. "I just about stepped on Alice."

Her hand was warm and soft and delicate in his, like a thin, hairless rat.

The green overalls boy was wearing slippers of cartoon trains. "That's Max. He's super cool." Max must have sensed he was being talked about. His eyes popped open and he pulled his thumb out of his mouth and rolled onto his back. "That a good sign," whispered Miss Nora into the Devil's ear. "You know what they say about waking a sleeping child, right?"

The Devil turned to her. Their faces were so close their noses nearly touched. There was cinnamon on her breath.

"No. What do they say?"

"It's a cardinal sin."

Miss Nora bent over and gently picked up the boy. "Upsy-daisy," she said, and kissed him on the cheek as he groggily looked around. Then she rubbed his back. For the first time ever, the Devil felt jealous of a one-and-a-half-year-old.

"Let's go wash your face and give that hair a brush. This nice man's chosen you for a special job this afternoon!"

Nice man. She'd called him a *nice man.* The Devil got goosebumps.

"We won't take long. And we won't be too far."

"Oh," Miss Nora cocked her head. "Hang on. I assumed… I mean, couldn't you do your thing right here? With all the toys and stuff around?"

"I would, but I'm afraid it might be disruptive. A bit, you know, unsettling for the other little ones."

"Right, right. I get where you're coming from now. And it's true. Kids do like their routines. Especially these little hellions."

The Devil nodded. "Lots of ideal locations in and around a building like this."

She handed Max over. The boy settled comfortably on the Devil's hip.

"His dad usually picks him up at 3:15. So you have my blessings with him until then."

"Great. That'll be more than enough time."

She cleaned Max up and packed his *Star Wars* backpack with a granola bar, a sippy cup and a spare diaper, just in case.

"You know, I'd go with you if I could. And be, like, your assistant. But…" she waved her hand over all her sleeping charges.

"Oh no. I'll be fine. I get it. You've got your job and I've got mine."

"Yeah. You're right. I really can't leave. So instead, I figured Miss Clare could go with you."

Miss Nora motioned toward a woman sitting in the corner in a rocking chair near Swimmy the Fish's bowl. She was scrolling through her phone from under long bangs. The Devil hadn't even noticed her before. "She's only part-time, but the kids love her. Max will feel super comfortable with her there, too."

The Devil hadn't counted on having a chaperone. He sucked in his breath. Miss Clare dropped her phone into her purse, shot the Devil a bored look and led the way through the cloakroom, out the double doors and into the community centre.

"Look," said Miss Clare when they were in the hall. "I don't know you from a hole in the ground, but I've been working since six thirty this morning. I'm dying for a smoke. Wait here, okay?"

Before the Devil could respond, the woman zipped out a side exit, and he was alone with the boy.

He bit the inside of one cheek to suppress a smile. Sometimes it seemed the heavens just lined up for him.

When the Devil finished the various secret rituals involved in the Dark Power Takeover of Max's soul, he blew out the candles, popped his paraphernalia back into his bag, changed the boy's diaper, unlocked the door and left the wheelchair-accessible washroom.

You might expect the child to start speaking in tongues he'd never learned in a voice of low baritone range, to spew blasphemies while his eyes rolled back in his head, to sprout a tail, to convulse in a fit of fury or to have a sudden, sinister, supernatural glow.

But that's not how it works.

It's true that the toddler's soul was officially possessed; he was an agent of Hell and everything he did from that moment on and throughout eternity would glorify Lucifer and strengthen the Empire of Evil. But from the outside he looked pretty much the same. And what child doesn't act like a wretched devil a good percentage of each day anyhow? Parents generally chalk it up to the terrible twos.

The Devil had a spring in his step as he and Max walked down the hall, and it wasn't just because of the fresh young soul he'd bagged, or the fact that this was proof it was possible—nay, easy!—despite what those lazy underlings claimed. No, he was on the ninth cloud because he was going to ask Miss Nora to go on a date. Maybe he'd suggest dinner at Chipotle. They had some new Habla Diablo spiced wings on the menu. He pictured her licking the drippy red sauce from her dainty fingers.

He hoisted the boy up onto his shoulders and put his hands on his shins to keep him steady. Max seemed to enjoy the ride. His pudgy hands, buried in the Devil's curly black hair, had found two tiny horns, and was "steering" with them. The Devil made *neeerrrooom neeerrrooom* noises, like wheels turning on a race-car track. They were having such fun, careening through the halls of the community centre, that the Devil lost track of where they were going. Before he knew it, they were in front of the seniors' lounge.

When the old people saw him again, they started yelling. "Please! Come help us! We've been waiting for you!"

He looked at the clock on the wall above the coffee maker. Only 1:45, still nap time. Max was having a great time. There was no rush to get back to Li'l Sprouts. Miss Nora would be there all afternoon.

Maybe it was because of Miss Nora's kindness toward him, or the fact that she seemed to be a kindred spirit. Maybe it was the time with the child, or the elation of completing the dark rituals. Cynics would say it was the prospect of getting laid that night. Whatever the reason, the Devil was in a good mood.

He decided to give the old farts a chance. *What the hell*, he thought. *Wouldn't kill me to do a good deed.* He knew that by granting a few dying wishes in exchange for their rusty souls, he'd be getting the raw end of the deal, but he headed for the seniors' lounge nonetheless.

"Duck!" he told Max when they went through the doorway.

The old people welcomed him with slobbering affection. Someone brought him a can of Coke, said it was nice he was participating in Bring Your Child to Work Day, reached up and gave Max a Sprite. Someone asked if it was okay if the boy had sugar. "Bring it on," said the Devil.

"I'm just grateful you're here," said an old woman in yoga pants, coarse grey hair bound by a scrunchie on top of her head. "Finally."

With a grunt, the Devil lifted the boy off his shoulders, then sat down, plopped his bag on the table in front of him and Max on his knee, and whispered to the boy to watch carefully. "I'll be working pretty fast here. Don't interrupt me." Max started chewing on the Devil's access pass.

"Well? Who wants to go first?" said the Devil. He took a sip of pop, blew on his hands, rubbed them together and rolled up his sleeves. Normally he procured souls in private, but everyone knows the elderly are used to humiliation and embarrassment. In his experience, they had very little pride. What would it matter if a few of their cronies looked on?

No one came forward.

"Despite what you may have heard, I don't have all of eternity here. Let's get this rolling."

For the next twenty seconds or so, the saggy elders just looked at each other with confused faces. All you could hear was the squeak of wheelchair tires on the linoleum as someone shifted his seat, the *puff puff puff* of oxygen going through a tube into someone's nose, and a bit of snotty snuffling from Max.

"So, um, *are* you the guy from Shaw?" said the man who had recognized him first.

"The who?"

Everyone started talking over one another.

"Our internet's been down since ten this morning. Someone was meant to come and fix the modem."

"Yeah. Tech said you'd be here an hour and ten minutes ago."

"Can you fix it or what?"

"Wait—what?" said the Devil. "Slow down."

"We're supposed to be live-streaming a webinar on navigating the increased airport security measures for international travel. A few of us are going to walk the Camino de Santiago next month."

"The modem is over there, next to the snack table."

"It's done this before. I think we need to change servers."

"Do you want a muffin? A tart?"

"He doesn't need a muffin. He needs to get to work."

"We don't need to change servers. It's not the server, it's the connection."

"Make room. Let the poor man think."

The Devil removed Max from his knee, stood up and adjusted his pants.

"Look," said the Devil. "I don't know thing one about fixing your internet." He was a little hurt and a little embarrassed. It was like when you asked an ugly girl out on a date because you felt sorry for her and she said no, she had other plans.

He scooped Max up, stormed out of the room and headed back to Li'l Sprouts. "Rule number one," he said to the child he bounced on his hip down the hall. "Follow your instincts and don't bother doing any good deeds." The boy yanked sideways so hard on the lanyard that the Devil choked on his breath.

A woman in the hallway past the gym looked up at them. "Jesus. There you are!" It was Miss Clare. "Are you done or what?" she said.

The Devil brushed by her without answering. Max reached out his hand. He wanted Miss Clare to carry him. The Devil held him tight, but the kid arched his back and nearly flung himself onto the floor.

"Fine. See if I care," said The Devil, plopping the child down so he could take Miss Clare's hand. Then the boy reached up and surprised the Devil by taking *his* hand on the other side. They walked three abreast past the gym and the cafeteria.

"Well don't you look like the happy family!" came a high, lilting voice. It was Miss Nora, peeking out from the Li'l Sprouts doorway far down the hall. She seemed to be surrounded by a halo of pulsing light.

"Ah, Jesus Christ," whispered Miss Clare. "Spare me."

The child's grip tightened.

"Swing me!" he shrieked. "Swing me super-duper high!"

The Devil was mesmerized by the vision of light and loveliness at the end of the hall.

There was no time to brace himself when Max suddenly hoisted both feet off the ground, yelled, "Wheeeee!" and hurled his legs forward gracelessly.

With the sudden tug, the Devil's shoulder just about popped out of its socket; he lost his balance and stumbled to the side. "Why, you little..." He swiped at the child but missed. His bag tipped open. A Mason jar full of silver powder, an ancient-looking leather-bound book with a burn mark on the cover, an old-fashioned, horseshoe-shaped magnet, a black velvet cloth, a silver turkey baster, a triangle of fur and a Bunsen burner spilled out onto the tile floor.

Miss Clare looked down at the paraphernalia. "Weirdo," she scoffed. "I knew you weren't really a photographer. C'mon Max. This dude's a freak." She walked with Max the rest of the way back to Li'l Sprouts, leaving the Devil rubbing his arm and reorganizing his things.

Weirdo? Freak? thought the Devil. *Internet repairman?* Maybe it was time to work on his image. Get a tattoo. Or a new pair of shoes.

The Devil's ego was bruised, but it was not broken. He spat in his hands, rubbed them together and smoothed his hair at the sides, then tucked in his shirt, hitched up his pants and walked back to Li'l Sprouts with his hands on his hips and his bag hanging casually off one shoulder.

The children were gathered around watching a cartoon about Noah's ark. Miss Nora was humming while she organized toys at the sand station. It was the perfect time to ask her out, but this was new for him. He was nervous. There was something in his throat that a poet might have said was his heart.

He stepped toward her.

She looked up.

The thing in his throat swelled.

"Oh, goody," said Miss Nora before the Devil could even open his mouth. "You're back." Then she held his hand like she was reading his palm, and gave him a small vial. "Here. Like I promised." She closed his fingers around the dark-brown bottle. "It's called RainForest Dew. It's a combination of sandalwood and tangerine essential oils. Perfect for helping your body retain its natural humidity."

"Wow," said the Devil. "I'm touched." He gulped. "Say, I was thinking, I mean, I'm wondering if—it might be nice—if you have no other plans tonight..."

"Oh, Stan—that's so funny! I was just about to ask you if you had any other plans tonight too!"

"Ha ha," laughed the Devil awkwardly. "I guess we're on the same wavelength."

Something in the playroom caught her eye and Miss Nora called out, "Ma—ax! No tapping on Swimmy's bowl. Get your hand out of there. Fishies don't like getting played with, honey. You know that."

Then, back to the Devil, and in an even sweeter tone: "Stan, from the moment you walked in here I had a feeling that you and I shared the same passion for life. Drive. Vision. You come across as a real striver. You're your own boss—obviously an entrepreneur. And with *a lot* of connections."

"I do travel in a number of circles."

"Please don't think I'm too forward, but I've been looking for a partner in this new and unique business opportunity. You seem just the type to dial in with me on a home-based venture that will guarantee eternal freedom and prosperity."

The Devil felt his mojo expand like puff pastry in a hot oven. "Partner?" he asked.

"Anyhow, I'm having a Make 'n Take this evening. A few of us are getting together at my place to learn about the healing powers of essential oils and how to build our financial future through network marketing. You'll leave with some household cleaners, bath oils and several delicious blends for your infuser. I think I saw an infuser drop out of your bag when you guys were in the hall—sorry to spy. I just have this feeling you'd be one hell of a natural at this. I've got a friend in Utah who's making like six figures and he just started last spring."

Miss Nora jotted down her address on the back of a scribbled-on dot-to-dot page. *See you tonight!* she wrote, with a little heart as the dot over the *i*.

If she could sign this Stan guy up, he would be the third new Gold Level Distributor on her team of Go-Getters in a month, making her eligible for the Living Abundance bonus of 250 dollars that would be e-transferred to her account from head office in Salt Lake City before the end of the next business day.

"Everyone's arriving around eight o'clock. Why don't you come a little early? We can get to know each other a bit better."

The Devil was over the moon. Miss Clare was rolling her eyes. Max was putting Swimmy the Fish in the front pocket of Alice's backpack. The real internet technician was tucking a zip-lock bag of butter tarts into his bag—a thank-you gift from the seniors for getting their WiFi up and running. Miss Nora was holding back a wicked grin as she calculated this month's earnings in her head.

And the demons back in Hell were arguing over what was taking the Devil so long and placing bets on whether he'd return at all.

Nasal Cannula

It takes a few minutes for Anton, Carmen's father, to lower himself into the driver's seat. He grabs the fabric of his beige pants with knotted fingers and hoists his thin legs up and around, licks his lips and stares straight ahead to the garage wall for a few moments. The valve on his new, small oxygen tank needs adjusting. Then he straightens out the tubes that allow him to suck pure oxygen into his failing lungs.

"Do you know what they call this?" he asks, waving the clear plastic tube in front of him.

"Your breathing thingamabob?" says Carmen.

"Nasal cannula. Nasal cannula!"

"Well. Learn something new every day."

"Pretty fancy name for 'tube poking up your booger-hole,' if you ask me," says Anton.

"Yup, pretty fancy. Sounds Latin."

"Sounds like a name you'd find on a tourism brochure of Venice. The Nasal Cannula."

"So romantic."

Carmen hasn't seen her father for six weeks. It's a short flight, but always complicated getting from Vancouver to Calgary; there's so much to organize—school events, rescheduling her own clients, making sure there's food in the fridge for Eduardo and the girls.

Anton's metal oxygen travel tank can be tucked inside his windbreaker. It's about the size of a large canister of whipping cream, in a protective case made of wetsuit material. It's not too heavy, but it weighs him down. He jokes that it makes him feel tough, like he's "packing heat." Like he's got a secret superpower. Carmen knows he hates it. Just like she knows he hates waking up at eleven fifteen a.m. after going to bed at eight thirty the night before. "Living the life o' leisure, I am. Early to bed, eventually to rise," he says. Her mother Bettina was the opposite. She needed less and less sleep as she aged. It's hard to die in your sleep when you're an insomniac, but she managed.

He turns the key then turns to Carmen: "Well m'lady, we haven't even left the castle and I've forgotten where we're going."

"McDonald's. Remember, Dad?" It depresses her that a trip to a fast food restaurant is a highlight of her father's day, perhaps his week, yet it still slips his mind. "Yes! That's right! Fine dining under the golden arches."

He tells her about his friend Lyle Fee who can't chew anything due to an operation to remove cancer from his tongue. "FeeFee loves Big Macs so much he puts them in the blender, adds a little water and drinks them through a fat straw."

Carmen makes a gagging sound.

"True story. I even tried a sip. Used my own straw though. You never know what kind of germs FeeFee's picked up."

"Stop," says Carmen. "I swear, I'll puke."

"Flavour's the same, solid or liquid. That's the McDonald's magic."

Carmen twists her face and rolls her eyes. The smoothies she makes for her family consist mainly of kale, blueberries, plain yogourt and almond milk. She's not the kind of mother who feeds her children fast food.

Anton shifts the silver Sunfire into reverse and jerks out of the garage. A neighbour is putting out recycling behind her garage. She waves, but Anton doesn't see her. Or, he does and ignores her.

There was a time when he would steer with his knees so he could rest his right hand on the stick shift and hang his left hand out the window, ready to give a thumbs-up or an A-okay sign to another driver or tap the beat of some song on the radio with his long, graceful fingers on the metal door of the old pickup truck. But those fingers are now crooked, the nails yellow and cracked. His cloudy eyes are watering as he squints into the rear-view mirror. Carmen knows he can't really see if there's anything coming from the side, but shoulder checking requires more flexibility than his body is capable of.

"Did I tell you Gracie got her *N*?" she says. "New driver's permit. She took sixteen hours of driver's ed classes, offered through her high school. Passed the driving test on her first try. She's really good. Careful, but confident. You would be proud of her."

He stops in the back alley, kitty-corner to the garage. If another vehicle came around the corner, it would T-bone the Sunfire.

"His son's trying to put him in a home."

"Who?"

"Lyle. Lyle's son's trying to take everything away. Lock him up."

"Well, I'm sure his son knows what's best. Maybe Lyle'd be happier there."

"Bull*shit*." He says it like the slamming of a door. Spit sprays the dashboard.

Carmen doesn't engage. Anton's mouth opens wide and he starts hacking. He clasps the steering wheel like he's a wide-eyed tourist leaning forward on a railing over some roadside pullout at a waterfall or a canyon, and coughs with such force Carmen winces, wondering if he might crack a rib.

She fiddles the tuning dial on the radio so he won't feel like she's waiting for him to stop, which he eventually does.

"Sure you're okay?" She turns the radio off and touches his leg with her fingertips. She means: *Are you sure you're okay to drive?*

He lifts his glasses and wipes his eyes. The plastic tubes look like laundry lines across his face, with two short prongs resting just inside his nostrils. "What do you call a masturbating cow?" he asks.

She raises one eyebrow.

"Beef stroganoff!" He starts coughing again.

"Dad. Seriously."

"So," he says when the hacking subsides. "A termite walks into a bar and says 'Hey! Is the bartender here?'"

His hands are shaking.

"Dad, we can just have lunch at home if you want."

"Get it? Is the bar *tender* here?"

"Yes! I get it. But Dad, if you're not feeling..."

He turns to face her directly. His face is splotchy. "Forget it. My dear, we are not cancelling. I have the finest table for two booked. I know the maître d' at Chez Ronnie's. I have a lunch date with my best gal." He pushes a button and flips the stereo to CD.

She's tired of his jokes. There are choices that need to be made. It's ridiculous for an eighty-two-year-old widower to be living alone in that big house. It's too much. It's time to sell the house, while he's still got his wits about him. He could move into an assisted-living home—somewhere with other seniors. Activities. Medical help when he needs it. Or he could move in with Carmen and Eduardo and the girls. They have the space. They've all agreed it would be great to have him around. She's here to plant the seed, open the conversation and start moving in the sensible direction.

But one thing is for sure: he should definitely not be driving. And she should not be sitting in the passenger seat, letting him. He could kill them both. All because she's the daughter and he's the dad and this is the way it's always been.

He shoves it into drive, but stays there with his foot on the brake and horks something from deep in his throat into a tissue.

"Mmmmm! Buried treasure," he says. "Wanna peek?"

"Oh my God, Dad. Gross."

He folds it neatly and stuffs it into a cup-holder.

Anton always used to drive a standard. It's what Carmen learned on in the parking lot of Southcentre, back when malls were closed on Sundays. "Four things any child of mine has to learn," he told her. "To start a fire with one match. Throw a perfect spiral. Make a nice hollandaise sauce. And drive a standard." The campfire, the football throw and the brunch special came easily; good driving with a stick shift and a sensitive clutch took many weekends. She remembers tears streaming down her face as he yelled at her for stalling the truck again and again. He told her if the engine fell out it would be her fault and he'd make her pick it up, carry it to Len's Auto Shop, wait there while it got fixed and pay for it with the next ten years' allowances.

His breathing finally steadies and the spurts of air through the tube regulate with his inhales. Each sip of oxygen reminds Carmen of a scuba diver exploring some unknown ocean. She imagines brightly coloured fish, puckered up as if coming in for a kiss, then swimming past, shimmering like satin windsocks. But it's quite the opposite. The *puff, puff, puff* from the medical tank is not a sound of freedom, but a reminder of her dad's weakening lungs, a symptom of his progressing disease. He's fairly stable now—the oxygen helps—but there's no denying the decline. His face is the colour of sand. His thin hair sticks to his head, like strings of dried alfalfa on an eggshell. He readjusts the tube and the clear plastic buds up his nose, buckles his seat belt and lurches out of the alley and onto Acadia Drive.

"Oh, wait! Did I shut that bloody garage door?" He presses the button that is attached with Velcro to the dash as he's driving away. "Or am I just opening it?" He presses it again, and again. "Bloody hell. Now I'm losing it. Your mom used to always close it. I control the car, she controls the garage door opener. It's probably going up and down like a bride's nightie right now."

He doesn't see the navy-blue SUV careen toward their car. The driver, in dark aviator glasses, throws one arm in the air, yells something. There's a woman in the passenger seat with her hands on her head and her mouth open. The driver lays on the horn and swerves around the Sunfire. There's a bus coming the opposite way and the SUV swerves back in front of Anton and Carmen to avoid it, missing the front end of the Sunfire by a whisper.

"Cheese and crackers!" says Anton. "Where did that *maniac* come from?"

"Dad! That 'maniac' had the right-of-way!"

She releases her grip of the dashboard. This would be a perfect opportunity to suggest maybe he's not the ace driver he used to be. Remind him that reflexes naturally slow as we age. Tell him how if he lived in Vancouver, Gracie could drive him wherever he needs to go. She would be delighted to be her grandfather's chauffeur. But taking away his licence would be taking away his freedom. He loves driving. To the hardware store. To the library. Out for groceries. To visit a friend. And, he often reminds her, he hasn't had an accident or a ticket in almost seventy years of driving. He also says he'd never move to Vancouver. He'd rather live in minus-thirty for half the year in a place he knows as home than be surrounded by yoga freaks and potheads where it rains thirty days each month, including February.

She says nothing. She cannot find the first words.

Driving with him through the neighbourhood she grew up in feels like an amusement park ride kicking into high gear, then having second thoughts and slowing down. Nausea envelops her. She clenches her teeth and folds her arms. She envisions the headline: *Vancouver Mother of Two and Elderly Father Die When Car Smashes into Woman's Former Junior High School: Province to review licensing requirements for seniors.*

He putters down Canyon Meadows Drive and onto Macleod Trail, singing along to some old Patsy Cline song. She's relieved it's an automatic; there's no way he could work a clutch. She isn't really sure what the government does about getting seniors tested.

Should she contact his doctor first? Tell him about her concerns? Is it something the police get involved in? What about his insurance? He shouldn't be singing. He's tapping his fingers, when he should be focused. But she admits to herself that he still has a pretty good voice.

"Beautiful colours this time of year," she says when the song's done. "Winter's coming."

"Need I remind you that it's only September? Still summer, technically. But yes dear, soon it will be fall. And then… cross-country ski season!"

Why is it so hard to bring up the obvious? He's sick yet insists he's fine. His diagnosis plus her mother's death has taken a toll, perhaps too quickly for him to even recognize what's happened. She wonders: could *he* still build a fire with one match? Throw a spiral? Make a hollandaise sauce? Doubtful. So why is driving still okay?

"You know Dad, Vancouver is really nice this time of year. In fact, there's green all year long."

"Oh! That reminds me. Why did the guy quit his job at the shoe recycling factory?"

"I don't know, Dad. Why?"

"It was sole destroying."

She purses her lips but a smile sneaks through.

"Atta girl," he says. *Puff puff puff.* "Say, what kind of sauce do I usually get with my McNuggets?" She's not sure if he's still in joke mode, or really asking. "What do I like? Is it honey mustard? Teriyaki? Sweet-and-sour?"

For years after her stroke, he'd bring his wife home a takeout Happy Meal every Friday. She'd pull the pickle off, eat the burger and half the fries, then put the McHappy toy in the kitchen drawer, beside the steak knives. The drawer is still full of the plastic trinkets and movie tie-in crap.

"I remember. It's barbecue! Mmmmmm. I do like barbecue sauce. I can almost taste it now." This is a man who was once the top emergency preparedness specialist for the provincial government. The man who brought the fire drill to Alberta schools. "What do I always say? Don't trust anyone who doesn't like barbecue sauce."

"Dad..."

"Don't tell your secrets to a honey mustard guy." *Puff. Puff. Puff.*

"You know..."

"Don't leave a sweet-and-sour man alone with your wife." *Puff.*

"Dad! I'm serious. We really think it's time you moved to Vancouver. Eduardo and I are worried about you. Gracie and Joy would love—we all would love it—if you moved in with us. We're your family. We'd like to be closer. There's the community centre just a few blocks away. Coffee shops. Bookstores. Vancouver has *everything*."

Anton's jaw tightens. His fingers whiten as he grips the steering wheel tighter.

Her voice is almost a whisper now. "I mean, it's either that or some kind of place where, like, for seniors. You know?"

There's a man standing on the side of the road. A hitchhiker. He leans lazily against a light post. His arm is bent, elbow at the ribs, thumb up, one foot resting against the post, like he really doesn't care if he gets picked up or not. It's an odd place to be hitching a ride, but Carmen doesn't give it much thought.

"Look, I just think we have to consider the options. Be realistic. Proactive. While you're still healthy enough to make smart choices and enjoy your life."

The man on the side of the road nods slowly as they approach.

They pass, and Anton's head suddenly swings around. He stares at the man on the road, mouth wide open, and his eyes brighten like he's found a one-hundred-dollar bill on the sidewalk. He veers across two lanes of traffic onto the shoulder.

"Shit, Dad! Watch out!" Carmen's purse falls off her lap onto the floor and the contents roll out. The driver they just cut off honks as he passes, and the passenger gives them the finger. Anton stops the car in a cloud of dust about one hundred feet ahead of the hitchhiker.

"Oh my God! What the hell are you doing?"

His eyes are stretched wide open. He adjusts the mirror and watches the hitchhiker saunter toward the car. "It's really him!" he whispers slowly. Then in a high-pitched crescendo, "I can't believe it!"

"Who? It's really *who*, Dad?" The hitchhiker is in his mid-twenties. Thirties, maybe. Face like a loaf of bread, rectangular, puffy and pale. Greasy black hair is smoothed back. He wears black pants, too short, and an untucked dirty white T-shirt that looks slept in. It's too small, rides up, cinches at the armpits. He is carrying nothing—not a backpack, shopping bag or even a bucket of water and a squeegee. His arms swing too high as he saunters casually to the car. Carmen has both hitched rides and picked up hitchhikers before; she knows it's part of the code to run, or at least walk quickly, when a potential ride stops.

"Do you *know* that guy?" she says, but her dad seems frozen, eyes glued to man in the rear-view mirror.

Then, as if he's been caught wearing a ball cap for dinner with the queen, Anton snaps out of his reverie, yanks the plastic tubes out of his nose and out from behind his ears and stuffs them in the inside pocket of his jacket beside the tank of oxygen. "Don't need this. Get it away. Okay. There. That's better," he mumbles. "How do I look?" His face has the same pleading need for approval that Gracie's had on her first day of high school.

"Dad! What's going on?"

Anton wipes a drip from his nose onto his sleeve, fumbles with a little box of Tic Tacs and pops one into his mouth.

"Carmy, be a dear and hop in the back," he says, crunching the mint.

"What?"

"Hurry. Get in the goddamn back seat! We need to show some respect to our guest." He pulls down the visor and looks at himself, checks his yellow teeth and smooths both eyebrows down. The wiry hairs will have nothing of it and spring back. Carmen doesn't move.

"I don't get it. Who...?"

"Out!" He is suddenly firm. She hasn't heard him speak to her like this since she was a teenager. "Now!"

"Since when do you even stop for..."

He clicks the *door unlock* button, grunts, reaches over her, across to the passenger side and pushes open the door. For a man who could barely breathe on his own just moments ago, he's surprisingly limber.

"G'won. Get out. Scoot, scoot," he says and shoves his adult daughter out of the car. She slaps his hands away.

"Jesus, Dad! What the hell?"

The hitchhiker is now beside the car. He takes a step back to make room for Carmen to get out.

"Ma'am," he says, and smiles. It sounds like "Myay-um." She is not impressed. He thrusts his hand forward to shake hers. She ignores it and smooths her skirt. He gives her a sleazy once-over, puts a pale, scrawny forearm on the door frame and leans into the car.

"I'm much obliged, sir," the stranger says to Anton. "Thank you for stoppin'."

"It's my pleasure. I've been hoping to find you."

All Carmen can think of is kicking him. Who the hell does this guy think he is? There's something familiar about his smile, lifted on one side into a flirty sneer, his sad-puppy eyes and the chin that seems too big for the rest of his face.

"Mighty kind of you to offer shotgun, ma'am," says the hitchhiker, "but I couldn't take a lady's seat." He opens the back door and steps inside. She notices his shoes: fancy blue penny loafers. No socks. They look ridiculous. She hopes he doesn't remove the shoes in the car; she already knows how they will smell. Carmen takes her place in the passenger seat again, and angrily picks up the contents of her purse.

Anton has one hand on his chest and thumps it, showing that his heart is racing. "Gosh, this is a great honour. Hope y'all haven't been waitin' long for me to pick y'all up."

"*Dad?* Why are you talking like that?"

Anton ignores her.

"Not at all," says the hitchhiker. "It's mighty fine weather to enjoy the out-of-doors."

Anton is beaming. His face has gone from dusty to rose.

"I'm sure you hear this all the time, but I'm a huge fan. The hugest. Always have been."

"Why, thank you. Thank you very much. I'm happy to hear it."

What the hell is going on? Carmen wonders. *A huge fan? Who is this guy?*

"Where're y'all headed?" Her dad has never been south of Seattle, and he's talking like he was born and raised in Memphis.

"Wherever *you* are," says the stranger. He leans forward between the seats and they laugh together at their own unfunny banter. His breath smells like garbage.

"All right then," Carmen snaps. "Would you please sit back and fasten your seat belt? It's been the law here for quite some time."

"Don't mind her," says Anton into the rear-view mirror. "You know women. If it's not one thing..." he shakes his head and smiles at the stranger in the back seat, who finishes the sentence with him. "It's another."

"We can drop you near McDonald's," says Carmen. "On Macleod Trail."

"McDonald's? Bless your soul. I love McDonald's!"

Oh my God. Please don't invite him to join us.

His head perches between the two front seats, and he looks back and forth between them.

Anton's fingers quiver on the steering wheel. "W-would you care to join us for a bite?"

"I'd be delighted, if y'all don't mind. However, I'm embarrassed to say I'm a little short on cash at the moment."

Carmen puts the palm of her hand on her forehead, her shoulder against the door. She suspects a migraine may be on its way.

"Say no more, friend," says Anton. "Hamburgers on us. Fries. Milkshakes. Whatever your pleasure, it would be our pleasure. It's not every day you go to McDonald's with the King of Rock 'n Roll."

Anton is still Anton: the hair sprouting from his ears has not changed, the skin on his throat still sags, but somehow he is no longer Carmen's father. His shoulders are no longer bony and hunched but pulled back, strong. His breath comes in mighty inhales and exhales, like a man standing at the bow of a ship, inviting pure ocean air to billow the sails of his lungs. He turns to Carmen; smiles and nods at her. One front tooth is chipped and the rest are stained beige and flat across the tops and bottoms from years of grinding, but his face pulls around them into a smile bigger than Carmen's seen on him in years. He clicks the turn signal, shoulder checks and smoothly pulls onto the road, merging seamlessly into the flow of traffic.

"Today. It's the kind of day that dreams are made of," says Anton. He rolls down his window and hangs his left arm out. "Now *this* is summer." He nods to the man in the back seat and winks at his daughter.

Her father has never winked at her in his life. She didn't think he even knew how. He never says anything is "what dreams are made of." If he didn't look so vibrant, she'd think he was having a stroke.

The hitchhiker offers him a cigarette.

"Uh... my father doesn't smoke," says Carmen.

"Such a nag!" says Anton. Then he pats her thigh like she's a dog, steering with his knees for a moment. "It's because she loves her old man."

"Actually," she says, removing his hand from her leg and putting it back on the steering wheel, "it's because you have a terminal lung condition, Father." She knows she's treating him like a child. It's the only way she knows how to maintain control.

"Oh, come on," chirps Anton. "Take a chill pill, sweetie-pie. It's a special occasion!"

"Jesus Christ. Out of the question," she hisses. And to the hitchhiker: "My father is *very* sick."

"Me?" Anton mocks surprise.

"It's his lungs."

"Such a pessimist."

"And his heart, his kidney. Not to mention his prostate."

Anton turns to the hitchhiker. "Don't mind Debbie Downer here." They both laugh and Anton takes the cigarette. "*Gracias, amigo!*"

"Dad, no! You are not sparking up a cigarette. There's an oxygen tank in the car. Think about that."

"Oh. Yes. You're right," Anton says. He raises his knees to the steering wheel, twists, turns and shimmies easily out of his windbreaker, rolls the lightweight jacket around the entire travel-tank breathing apparatus and the bundle of tubing, and lifts it to toss out the window. Carmen reaches across him and grabs it, stuffs it under her seat.

"Have you lost your mind?" she whisper-screams. "Pull over. Now. You're not fit to drive."

"Oh, hey. Have you heard the one about the guy who worked at the calendar factory?"

"Dad. Stop. Pull over."

"He got the sack for taking a couple of days off."

The hitchhiker laughs and gives Anton a squeeze on the shoulder. "Good one, man!"

Carmen heaves a sigh. At least the car isn't weaving.

"Oh! How rude of me," says the hitchhiker. "Debbie?" He offers Carmen a cigarette as well.

She rolls her eyes, clicks her tongue against the roof of her mouth and crosses her arms. He pulls out a lighter. Anton turns his head and arches backwards so the hitchhiker can light it.

"Oh my God. Watch where you're going!" Carmen grabs the wheel to steer. Anton puffs a few times, until the cigarette is fully lit. She waits for the inevitable cough, but it doesn't come. "I don't believe it. How long has it been since you quit smoking? What would Mom say?"

The man finally sits back and fastens his seat belt.

Anton doesn't really inhale the smoke, but lets the cigarette dangle from his lips. Somehow the smoke makes him look younger. "I can't believe it either! Your mother would have loved this!"

"I doubt that."

He looks for an ashtray, but there isn't one, so he drops the barely smoked cigarette into a takeout coffee cup that's been in the console for several days.

When they arrive at McDonald's, Anton and his rock 'n roll hero lope past the counter and the condiments station and the high chairs, straight to the PlayPlace in the corner, where a slide, a plastic table made of spinning *X*s and *O*s and some plastic tunnels await them.

"You can't go in there," yells Carmen. But neither of them weighs more than an average teenage boy, and she sees no sign indicating an age limit.

She waits in line to place their orders. Her father's oxygen tank and tubes are wrapped in the windbreaker under her arm; she knows he'll need them soon. In fact, perhaps he'll need paramedics soon. She watches Anton follow the man up the slide. His khaki slacks creep down in the back, exposing blue and grey checkered boxers underneath. They are both inside the yellow tube slide at the top. Carmen can see the silhouette of them rubbing each other's hair and hears them laughing about the way the static makes the strands stand straight up. The shadowy mass of men squirms farther down the slide, then stops just before the opening. The hitchhiker screeches. Says his shoulder is stuck. He can't move.

Anton is laughing so hard the entire PlayPlace seems to shake. Carmen envisions needing the jaws of life, usually reserved for rescuing people from car wrecks, to cut through the hard plastic and pry them out. They manage to free themselves and their bodies tumble out onto the floor, where they lie tangled together for a moment, then climb up the plastic stairs on the side, panting, faces sweaty and red, and yell "Hey! Hey! You! Look at us!" from a platform made to look like a pirate ship.

If it were two children, she would smile at their playful antics. But this isn't funny. Carmen cannot bear to acknowledge them. She places their orders and scans the empty restaurant. Shouldn't there be a store manager somewhere, telling them to leave? She's starting to sweat. There is an ache in her chest and she feels short of breath. Her head pounds. An aura begins to cloud her vision and she grabs the counter beside a plexiglas display case of hot apple turnovers.

"Lady? Lady? Hey! Are you okay?" says a clerk. "I can bring your food to you if you want to take a seat. It'll just be a few minutes."

Carmen drops into a corner booth and looks around the McDonald's, which is in need of a renovation.

Across the tables, a tall man with wavy silver hair mops

the floor. He doesn't seem to notice the two grown men in the PlayPlace slide-tube. If he does, he doesn't care. Why does it bother her so much? She puts her father's windbreaker on the bench beside her. The oxygen tank rolls out, but she catches it before it hits the floor. Sets it on her lap. Examines the apparatus. She's heard pure oxygen is quite the stimulant. Apparently the two short prongs work with the patient's own breath, enhancing their inhalations rather than forcing air in, as she had assumed. She puts the plastic nasal prongs against her cheek to see if she can feel any air blowing through. Nope.

"Your order?" says the clerk, setting the food on Carmen's table. She tucks the medical device quickly out of the way, dumps all three orders of fries onto the brown tray and shakes two tiny packets of salt over the pile. She organizes the packages—McNuggets, burgers, shakes, an oriental chicken salad for herself.

She tries to catch Anton and the hitchhiker's attention, to call them over for lunch, but they're back in the slide and don't hear her. The food will get cold. She should go over there and get them, bang her palm on the outer shell of the play structure, make them put their shoes back on and come eat. But right now she just feels tired. She doesn't want to deal with them.

She pinches three fries and files them into her mouth like love letters into a shredder, then picks up the nasal cannula again and turns the tube between her fingers while she chews the salty starch sticks. She raises the stiff plastic prongs toward her nostrils and inhales sharply. *What would it feel like to take just a little suck of pure oxygen?* she wonders. A little hit. It's natural. Pure. Surely it can't be *harmful* for a healthy person to get a little extra of life's essence. She wonders if her mother ever tried the oxygen from his tank.

She knows it probably won't work unless the prongs are stuffed right up inside her nose, but she's squeamish. She digs through the zipper compartment that holds the tank and finds a spare nose piece, wrapped in plastic. She's seen her dad do it enough times, it's easy to replace the used nostril tube. There's no one around, only that janitor whose back is to her, so she tentatively lines up the prongs right under her nostrils. Even though it's a new nosepiece, it feels like she's drinking from someone else's straw, or using their toothbrush, and the backs of her legs feel jittery. But she's curious, and it might make her head feel better, so she stretches her front lip down to widen her nostrils, and pushes the plastic nubs up into the middle of them, closes her mouth and draws in a smooth, deep breath. She is hit with an instant buzz, like champagne poured directly onto her brain, like nicotine to a non-smoker. The colours of the restaurant become brighter. There is a sizzle to the blood running through her veins, and it causes an inner vibration down to the arches of her feet and to the tips of her fingers.

She feels a need to move, so reaches for more french fries. The taste is pure ecstasy. Eyes shut, she slowly chews, then inhales, long and loud, sucking through her nose, through the tube, through to the pure source. She counts to ten, then exhales. These fries are the best things on the planet. Oh, how she's yearned for them! She starts eating them, two by two, with both hands, right, left, right. How has she never experienced fries like these?

She opens her eyes and the tall man mopping the floor is pushing his equipment past her booth toward the washroom. He looks at her as he passes and there is a moment, a pause and a smile. There's something so familiar to Carmen in his walk; in the way his mouth turns up on one side more than the other; in his eyes, turned down slightly at the corners. She struggles to place it—she knows she's seen this man somewhere before.

His back is to her table when it clicks: Thomas Miller. Her crush all through high school. Not her "official" date for grade twelve grad, but the one she danced with most of the night. His locker was next to hers. He bought her a giant chocolate chip cookie the day she got cut from the volleyball team.

She yanks the tubes from her nose as he sets a triangular sign on the floor outside the men's room door announcing that it is being cleaned. She tucks the breathing apparatus beside her on the plastic bench. Her hands shake as she tears open the salad dressing pouch with her teeth and her father and the hitchhiker come to the table.

They eat in silence.

Anton keeps stealing glances at the hitchhiker.

Carmen's eyes are on the door of the washroom where her high school sweetheart scrubs the toilets.

The hitchhiker's only focus is the food in front of him. When he's finished, he stands up, burps, hikes up his sweat-pants, thanks Anton for the ride and the meal, nods his head Carmen's way and walks past the bright plastic Ronald, out the automatic doors and down the street.

Anton looks tired. His eyelids droop and the skin under his jaw seems to have stretched. Carmen wonders if he might cry. There is dipping sauce on his cheek. Carmen asks him if he's going to finish his lunch. He mutters something, frowns and pushes the tray away. He pats his pants pocket and says he can't find his wallet.

"Seriously? I knew it," says Carmen. "That guy was a thief. How much cash was in it? And all your ID?" She darts out the door of the restaurant, but too much time has passed. There are too many directions a person could walk and she has no idea which way the man went. He's long gone.

Anton says he doesn't remember if there was any cash. He thinks probably all his ID was in it. He thinks it was brown, but it might be black. They look around the restaurant. Carmen checks through the PlayPlace. She looks up the slide, peers behind the pirate ship platform and under the *X*s and

*O*s table. No wallet. Perhaps Thomas Miller found it while he was cleaning. She'll have to go and ask him.

This isn't how it's supposed to go, she thinks, standing outside the men's room, next to the garbage can with the swinging *THANKS!* for people who dump the uneaten food and wrappers off the trays. *It's all wrong.* She hears a toilet flush, then the squirt of a spray bottle, and the squeak of the mirror being cleaned.

Is she embarrassed for him? Didn't he want to become a lawyer? What happened? She feels ashamed of her own snobbery. Her father is now walking toward the exit with the car keys in his hands. Is she embarrassed for the scene he and the hitchhiker made? Or for the oxygen tubes he saw her breathing with?

She wants to explain to Thomas that she's healthy. That she's doing great. She's on an adult women's soccer team. She's got her own financial consulting business and a couple of wonderful kids. She spins the wedding ring around her finger, shakes out her hair and waits. It's all under control.

Carmen catches up to her dad in the parking lot. Anton has the cannula in his nostrils again. The travel tank is tucked inside his jacket. He is slow and hunched as they cross the pavement. His feet barely shuffle; the effort of lifting his legs is almost more than he can manage now.

She holds his elbow tenderly.

When the janitor had finally emerged from the washroom, she'd asked him if he'd seen a men's leather wallet that may have been dropped in the restaurant somewhere. What she wanted to say first was, "Do you remember me, Tommy?"

"So sorry. Haven't seen one today," he'd said in a strong British accent. It wasn't Thomas Miller after all. They had completely different noses. Thomas Miller's eyes were blue. This man's were brown. She didn't know how she could have confused them. She shrivelled and left the restaurant.

A few more steps to the Sunfire and Anton stops. “Hey, kiddo. What did the zero say to the eight?”

“C’mon, Dad. Let’s just go.”

“Nope. Not even close. But I’ll give you one more guess.”

“I’m driving home.” Carmen is firm.

Anton passes her the keys without hesitation, then says, “Nice belt.”

She lets herself chuckle and gets into the Sunfire. She adjusts the mirrors and peeks back to see if she can catch a glimpse of the man she’d thought was Thomas Miller. Anton lowers himself gingerly into the passenger seat. He looks around, mutters that maybe the hitchhiker still needs to get someplace.

In the console between the seats lies Anton’s wallet. It is indeed brown. After checking that nothing is missing, Carmen pulls out of the parking lot and they take the long, slow route home. It’s quite possibly the first time Anton has sat in the passenger seat with Carmen at the wheel since the days he taught her to drive a standard at Southcentre Mall.

All the way home they both look at strangers on the sidewalk and talk about which is worse: dry cold, or rain.

The Maternal Instinct of Witches

One way for a witch to amuse herself, when the usual avenues of entertainment have been exhausted, is to have a child.

Why not? As a rule, witches don't have regular jobs, and they don't have friends. They are not interested in physical fitness or tidiness. They don't have hobbies, or watch television, or enjoy music, or travel. And there are only so many spells one can cast.

Yes, witches cook, but they never clean up after themselves. They just use the same dirty pots for the next day's meal. There's no garbage or compost to worry about either. If the scraps, peels, rotten ends, bones and other sharp bits aren't needed, they are given to the cat, whose name is usually Thunder. Poisonous parts are put in jars for safekeeping.

Everyone knows having a baby can be very, very good for getting a lady out of a rut, for breaking up routine when life begins to feel same old, same old.

Besides, getting pregnant is no big deal for a witch. When she is ready, she simply wraps a piece of thin white satin around the base of one of her skin tags. (Oh, there are plenty of dangling little beauty warts to choose from—over her eyebrow, between her breasts, in the armpit area...) She pulls the ribbon tight, ties a double fisherman's loop, pours herself a glass of vinegar—known among witches to prevent morning sickness—and waits.

Within a few hours, the skin tag, at first the size of an engorged tick on a dog, begins to swell and pulsate. Pulsate and swell. Soon it grows to the size of a peanut. Two tiny dots become visible near the top. These are the eyes. And behind them, under skin like wet rice paper, a wee oyster of a brain. Little flippers appear—the hands and feet. And if you look closely at this growing nugget, you may see what looks like a small black fist in the middle of the body, squeezing and pumping like it's preparing to punch someone's lights out. That's the baby witch's heart.

The pregnant witch lies quietly on her bed for the whole next day as her skin tag grows and morphs and grows some more. It is still attached to her body, but now it is kicking and twisting and jerking around. "Whoa there, cowgirl," says the witch. "This one's gonna be a handful!"

Tradition dictates the blessed mother-to-be wait until the witching hour to give birth. When both hands on her old grandmother clock point straight up, she gives the ends of the white satin ribbon a sharp tug, and with a hiss, a pop and a crunch, severs the connection between herself and her parasitic offspring. The process is actually quite neat and tidy. After releasing about a quarter of a cup of minty afterbirth, the hole where the skin tag used to be closes up like a sphincter. And the shiny white ribbon that initiated the pregnancy holds the child's hair up in a cute topknot.

The baby witch grows quickly, and makes a lot of noise. Of course, the mother witch does not feed it, because she is teaching it to be self-sufficient right off the bat.

Unlike other children, babies of witches are born with mouths full of teeth as sharp as foxes', pubic hair in all the normal places, the ability to speak three or four languages and the urge to flee.

But the best part of witch motherhood is watching the youngster try to find its way out of the home. "Ha!" cackles the witch. "Good luck, lassie!" For there is no door in the house, and the only windows are un-openable, with panes of shatterproof glass. Everyone knows witches fly up their own chimneys if they ever have to leave the house. But the child doesn't know that... yet.

The mother witch laughs until she cries as the child crawls, and scratches, then climbs, jumps and even tries to fly to escape. *She looks like a hen in an elevator*, thinks the mother witch, wiping slippery tears off her cheeks.

The more desperate the child witch is to get out, the more hilarious it is to watch. This doesn't mean the witch doesn't love her child. Quite the opposite. Love in witches equals novelty plus narcissism, and a frantic child who has the same nose as you offers both!

However, in every life there are difficult decisions to be made. If the child witch doesn't figure out how to escape soon, the mother witch will know it is weak and feeble-minded, and she will roast the little thing in her oven and feed it to the cat, who is now sharpening his claws in mouth-watering anticipation.

Oh, don't judge.

A mother bird will shove her baby out of a high, high nest and watch as the terrified creature flails and spins and tries to figure out how to outsmart gravity before *thunk*ing onto the ground and smashing its itty-bitty birdie bones into smithereens. It's called *parenting*.

If the young witch *does* figure out how to escape, and zips into the fireplace and up the chimney flue, the mother witch will go back to cracking her knuckles, spying on her neighbours and reading spell books. "That was fun," she'll say, then pour herself another glass of vinegar, also known to prevent postpartum depression and empty nest syndrome.

Deep down she'll be of two minds. Partly, she'll be relieved to have her own life back, along with all that free time and privacy. Partly she'll miss the noise.

And as the child flies out the chimney, over the rooftops and into the night, she'll be so happy to be free she'll yank the white ribbon out of her hair and throw it gleefully into the air. It will crackle and flash in the sky. People below will stop what they are doing and look up at the lightning bolt. Only a few will be aware that this is a signal that a child witch has escaped. Most people will chalk it up to a freak storm on an otherwise lovely evening.

A few moments later, the ear-splitting growl of a witch's cat will send shivers up and down the people's spines. It seems Thunder sharpened his claws for nothing.

Crumble

Karina takes notes. It helps her keep a handle on things. She has Tyler's temper and moods down to a science, and she records her observations in an old spiral-bound notebook from her grad student days. She recognizes that her husband is prone to periods of rage and she has broken these episodes into five stages:

Stage 1: Trigger. Technically, the trigger cannot be considered a "stage" in itself, as it is simply the initiating force for the episode. Approx. duration: n/a (sudden, unpredictable).

Stage 2: Blame/Rant. May or may not be directly related to trigger. Predominantly verbal. Involves accusations directed at K. Verbal tone: rude. May or may not include obscenities. Approx. duration: 15 minutes.

Stage 3: Buildup. T abruptly stops blame/rant dialogue and sits quietly, usually at the kitchen table, fuming. Breathing becomes short and audible. Face flushed. Passive, yet tense. Buildup of aggression. Approx. duration: 12–30 minutes.

Stage 4: Rage. Predominantly physical. Potentially violent. May or may not involve stomping of feet and slamming of doors/cupboards. Fists clenched. Potential weapons may or may not include knives, shovel, hammer, barbecue tools, golf clubs, blankets, garden shears and other hand-held tools. Approx. duration: 30–40 minutes (or until collapse).

Stage 5: Denouement. Involves contrition/retribution (characterized by statements indicating shame such as *I love you*, *You are my world*, *Let's get a sitter and go out for dinner*, etc.) or direct self-reproach. Approx. duration: varies, 15 minutes to several weeks.

In other words, Karina knows what to expect and this allows her to prepare. Keeping a record of his bad spells, a history of his losses of control, helps her with the Three *P*s: Predict, Prepare and Protect herself against upcoming incidents. She knows when to pull the blinds down in the living room and when to tuck the girls out of harm's way. Her work at the lab has taught her the value not only of documentation, but of privacy and safety.

Anne says the notebook will come in handy when authorities have to be called in. Karina feels Anne makes a big deal out of things. She doubts it will come to that. She tells Anne everything is under control.

Anne, a neat freak, a widow and a size two, tells her not to be so sure.

On this particular day, Stage 1 and Stage 2 do not indicate any signs out of the ordinary. *T accuses K of seeming tired*, she writes under *Trigger*, referring to herself in the third person as a strategy to remain objective. "You look tired. Are you having one of those days?" he had said out of the blue while they were clearing the table. "I can do the girls' baths tonight. Why don't you chillax?"

Had she yawned during dinner?

Were there dark circles under her eyes?

Karina knows that the trigger can appear meaningless, but she understands it through the analogy of an electric switch. Women like Karina and Anne are familiar with switches. Then for twelve minutes after the trigger, Tyler verbally lashes out. He says it's "no wonder" she's so darn tired. Questions whether it's normal for children as old as three and four years old to still wake up during the night. Suggests she think about cutting down on her hours at the lab so she can have more energy and time to do the things she used to enjoy before they had children. Cruelly, he lists them: going to movies with friends; playing piano; going to the gym.

Anne: *He really said that? He really told you your career is a waste of time? He said you need to start getting some exercise? Unbelievable.*

Once he enters Stage 3 (Buildup), Karina sneaks into the laundry room, sits on the floor with her back against the dryer to record the details of the previous stage in her notebook as she remembers them. She knows that Anne doesn't need notebooks anymore. She doesn't have to worry about predicting, preparing for or protecting against this kind of thing. Her girls, the same ages as Nina and Molli, have done fine, even without their bio-dad around. She closes the notebook, holds it against her chest and creeps around the corner, the pencil clamped so tightly between her teeth she feels flecks of orange paint chip off.

Tyler's sitting at the kitchen table, clearly deep into this dangerous middle stage, staring out the window. He cracks his knuckles then rubs the back of his neck. Karina shudders. It appears that not only does he feel his wife is an overweight, out-of-shape failure and a bad mother, intentionally committing insomnia, but her pathetic, full-time, underpaying job gives him a sore neck.

He doesn't look up when he says, "That crumble smells great. Hope there's ice cream to go with it."

Karina braces herself. There isn't any ice cream. She gulps. She already knows what Anne has to say: *Think about it, Karina: he wants to have his cake and eat it too. With ice cream! It's that sense of entitlement that so often leads to violence.*

Instinct takes over and she knows what she needs to do. She moves through the kitchen like a ghost and doesn't exhale until she reaches the downstairs playroom. "Come on, Nina. Don't drag that blanket. Hurry, Molli," she whispers, shuffling them upstairs, out the back door and around to the side of the house to the driveway in the front. She glances back at the two-tone split-level as they climb into the truck and takes a mental picture in case nothing's ever the same again. The girls' bikes are splayed across the lawn. *Molli Rools* is scrawled in sidewalk chalk beside one crumpled sock, a skipping rope and an empty yogourt tube. Karina imagines a black-and-white photo of the house as it would look on the front page of the newspaper. She puts her daughters in their car seats.

"We wanna go back inside," says one.

"Yeah! We were playing in Play Tent Princess Castle. Where are we going?"

Far. Take them far away.

"Nowhere," says Karina. "Not yet."

They stop whining when she hands them each their electronic games and wraps the *Beauty and the Beast* fleece blankets around their legs. Quickly hypnotized, they huddle together in the back seat and start clicking. Their faces are almost identical, like hand-painted porcelain dolls. She imagines what they will look like when they are older, and how they will be taken advantage of for their beauty. She tells them to stay put no matter what. She starts to explain how too much of something called testosterone can make daddies a little cuckoo, but that he still loves them; she tells them she hopes when they are older they will remember what she has taught them about remaining in control of their own lives, and always standing up for themselves, each listening to that little voice inside her head that tells her what to do. But they don't care. They're immersed in *Animal Jam*, their safe, predictable online world. Karina knows that Anne would have given her children books, not devices.

She closes the truck door quietly, clicks the lock button on the fob, and casually re-enters the house as if she's just come back from checking the mail. Then she hides the keys in one of her boots at the back of the closet. She knows better than to put them into her own pants pocket, where he could shove his dirty, meaty hand and grab them. She checks the hook for the spare set but doesn't see it.

Karina holds her breath and peeks around the corner again. Tyler is still sitting at the kitchen table hunched over, locked in Stage 3. This is her window of opportunity. She should start packing. She should stuff two backpacks with everything the girls need for the week at preschool. Her lab coats are already at work—they are washed nightly by the research centre's linen service. She hesitates, then hears Anne's words: *A leopard can't change his spots. Unless he's no longer a leopard.*

Tyler's shoulders and back heave with each wheezy breath, and his bald head shines under the light. She checks her notes and her watch. It's been nearly forty minutes of silence. Before this, the longest he's ever been in Stage 3 was on May 19 of last year when, after twenty-nine minutes of silence, he slammed his palms on the table, stood up suddenly and unleashed an epic half-hour Stage 4 of domestic vandalism that included cleaning the barbecue with such force he broke the bristle brush, dumping a basket full of freshly washed laundry onto the bed and aggressively folding it, and pruning the lilac bush far more than was necessary. She didn't think the bush would ever blossom again.

The girls were two and three years old at the time. Impressionable. Vulnerable.

How long are you going to let this go on? Anne doesn't even have to say it. *When are you going to take control of your life?* Anne thinks Karina is weak. Brave Anne, with her tidy yard, skinny jeans and clever, polite, literate children.

But what if he's *not* a monster? Karina considers going to him, rubbing his shoulders and telling him everything is going to be okay, offering him some rhubarb crumble while it's still warm. It is an instinct she recognizes and ignores. Anne wouldn't hear of it.

A cast-iron frying pan sits on the counter. It would be so easy to lift it high above her head and bash it down onto his skull while he's sitting there. In self-defence. She imagines the vibration tingling up her arms and throughout her body like an orgasm.

Now you're thinking! It would feel so good! And you have those notebooks, for proof. Evidence.

Perhaps today's extended Stage 3 will mean an abbreviated Stage 4, thinks Karina in a burst of optimism. Maybe there will just be a little exasperated sighing and some fluffing up and punching down of pillows, some anger-fuelled rearranging of patio furniture. Then, after expunging the rage, he will quickly move into something passive-aggressive, like, *Hey! Let's go camping this weekend*, or *Talked to your mother lately?*—a typical bridge to contrition. At this point, it would be safe for Molli and Nina to come back inside. It would only be a bit past bedtime. The whole family could have dessert together and he'd finally move beyond the whole ice cream issue.

Tyler has never used the word "sorry," per se. He has other ways of making it up to her. It might be the next day, or it might be days, weeks, even a month or more after one of his episodes. But eventually she knows she can count on at least a gesture he deems apologetic. Maybe he'll text the lab while she's trying to work—something about being the luckiest guy in the world. A bouquet of roses might arrive: *Special delivery for Karina Bellingham*, the card would say. *Just 'Cause I Love You*. She would leave them with Mei-Ling at reception. He knows fresh flowers are not permitted in her work area, but he never remembers. She looks back through her notebook: a new pair of boots (half a size too big); a box of Rogers' chocolates (a repeat gift from the year before).

Anne tells Karina she's a sucker to fall for these trite gestures. She says Karina fits all the stereotypes and doesn't talk to her for few days.

Karina considers creating a spreadsheet on her computer to more specifically and accurately track Tyler's episodes of abuse and retribution—instead of the old spiral-bound notebook. Lately, the laptop has been used exclusively for her research on mucosa-associated bacteria in the human gastrointestinal tract. Microbes that live within us and could flourish into colonies of disease at any moment. But there's something about putting pen to paper in a notebook that makes it more—what? immediate? intimate?—than a spreadsheet.

Karina sits on the stairs by the back door, listening, knees pressed against her chest. Waiting for him to blow up is like living near the train tracks. At first you can't sleep, waiting for the whistle to scream, for the metal wheels to screech against the rails. And after a while, your heart doesn't jump at the sound. You know exactly when it will happen. You might not open your eyes anymore when it passes in the darkness, and you might not even notice when they change the train schedule altogether.

But Karina still notices.

It's now been a full forty-six minutes of Stage 3. This is unprecedented—he's taking too long and her breathing is coming in shallow puffs. She holds her pen on the paper and draws a crooked line to the bottom of the page, like a fault line on a seismological map. The foreshadowing of an earthquake. This is what it's like to live on the San Andreas. She flips through her notes and compares dates, times, triggers, responses, looking for patterns and irregularities.

There are always patterns, even in unpredictability, says Anne. As a scientist, Karina already knows this. She scans the pages quickly.

She hears a little movement from the kitchen. He calls her

name, twice.

She doesn't move. He sounds calm. His voice inflects a little uptick at the end of her name. It terrifies her.

She hears some shuffling around, then his heavy footsteps. He's looking for her. He's getting desperate.

Stage 4.

For a moment Karina thinks, *What if I just obeyed him?*

Anne would be disappointed, sure, but maybe if Karina went back to doing more of the things she used to enjoy, everything would be better. Maybe she should do what he says: call some of her girlfriends for a night of dancing at Blue Tribe, or go to the gym and take a spin class. Why not? Get out her old Royal Conservatory piano books.

Silly woman! What would that solve? Of course, Anne was listening. *You know he'll find a way to twist it around. Remember last time?*

How could she forget? A few months ago. Something from her old Scott Joplin collection: "Maple Leaf Rag." That was all the trigger he'd needed.

Remember how he mocked you? Humming along, sweeping Molli off of the floor, spinning her around the room and nearly smashing her skull on the ceiling as he "danced" with her?

It all comes back to her. Molli's shriek had been bloodcurdling. Nina had pulled at his pant leg as if to say, "Stop, Daddy! You'll kill her!" and then he did the same thing to the older girl. When Karina could no longer bear it, she closed the piano lid, pulled the distraught girls away and locked them in the crawlspace under the stairs while she prepared for Stages 2 through 5.

No, she thinks. *Anne's right: with an unstable man, there will always be another trigger. There will always be a next time.*

What Karina really wants is to fast-forward through the next part and go to bed, where she will definitely not have sex with him. Tomorrow, perhaps, and even then she will only nominally participate. But not tonight. Never the night of.

There are always repercussions. It is an unspoken matter of control—she'll make him wait until she feels in control again. She'll wait for the go-ahead from Anne.

The front door opens and shuts. Then, a car door. The roar of the truck's diesel engine.

Fuck.

Karina's gut tumbles and she scrambles to the front window. *Now he's done it,* says Anne. *I told you something like this would happen, didn't I? But you didn't listen. You didn't get out when you still could. And now it's too late. You never listen to me. Stupid, stupid, stupid woman.*

Block her out, thinks Karina, and checks her boot in the back of the closet. The keys are still there. Shit! She forgot about the kitchen junk drawer. The spare set.

You forgot?

Thrusting open the front door, she steps outside into a cloud of exhaust. The truck careens around the cul-de-sac. She sees the tailgate, the red rear lights, then nothing. She stares down the silent street. There is no precedent for this.

Ha! I knew it. I told you. So now what are you gonna do? Run after them? Throw your little notebook after them?

When Karina can no longer hear the sound of the engine, she feels like an air traffic controller after the whole sky has gone blank. There is a wind-up monkey in her chest, pounding on a tiny drum, too fast. *Rat-a-tat-tat. Rat-a-tat-tat.*

There is the scent of freshly cut grass. And someone having a barbecue.

She can't tell if her feet are on the ground anymore. She might be floating away.

A baby cries. A dog barks.

Finally she exhales, goes back inside, shuts the door gently behind her and walks into the kitchen in a trance. She is still holding the notebook.

There's pasta—buttered, with parmesan cheese—in Molli's

small bowl beside the sink. She twists the fork and takes a bite. It's cold but soft, so she takes another. And another.

She should make some calls. Who? The police? What would she say? What if she had to hand over her notebook? Is she ready? Is this how it will end? Will Molli and Nina ever forgive her?

She closes her eyes and feels the rhythm of her own chewing. The tasteless starch has precedence. When she swallows, it's like putting a cool cloth on a fevered forehead. The monkey settles, his manic drumbeat slows. She finishes the noodles then looks around. *Your little girls are gone. A man with a documented history of potential violence, currently in Stage 4, is on the highway with innocent children in the vehicle.*

Anne loves drama. Karina needs time to think.

And all you can think to do is eat?

Karina finishes the second bowl of pasta and her breathing calms. It's as though she's opened the front door and there stands a dear old friend who knows just what to say and what not to say.

The rhubarb crumble, straight from the pan: it's sweet and moist and it cradles her in a beautiful, soft, oatmeal, butter, brown sugar and cinnamon embrace. She doesn't swallow one bite before opening her mouth for the next. Her mouth, her throat, cannot be empty. Her tongue cannot be dry.

Anne is cheering her on now. *You're so good at this! See? You really are good at something.*

Did he take his wallet? She looks beside the stereo where he usually leaves it. Not there.

Of course it's not there. Did you really think...?

When the crumble is almost gone, she pops two frozen waffles into the toaster. In the meantime, there's bread. She pulls the soft part out of the centre, throws the crust in the sink and slathers the pillowy middle with butter. Water along with it. Spies Nutella. Digs the butter knife in, licks it off. One bite of bread, one bite of chocolate-hazelnut spread. Saves time by not spreading it on. Looks for ice cream to pave the way. Remembers: none. Right. It's okay, drink something. Move on. Waffles ready. Pizza Pop in the microwave.

She should have sent the girls to the neighbours' place. Should have guarded the door.

Told you so.

Another Pizza Pop. The counter is strewn with food, dishes, crusts. She should have gone outside earlier. Should have left with them when she had the chance. Gone anywhere.

Shoulda woulda coulda.

Alpha-Bits in the pantry. She pours a bowl of breakfast literature. It's all she can do. Milk splashes over the side. Bends over and eats half, barely chewing. Opens cupboard doors. She knows she should check if the girls' passports are still in the cedar box in the den, but she is afraid of what she will discover.

You're chicken, that's what you are.

Chips!

But don't ask what flavour they are. Sour cream and onion? She doesn't even like that kind. Doesn't matter. This is a different kind of hunger: it has nothing to do with taste or appetite. Like how sex has nothing to do with love. She tears into the other waffle, tasting nothing, stuffing it in. Finishes the cereal. Drinks the milk from the bowl. What is she without her stuffing? An empty, flattened box? An outline on the pavement? It's been sixteen minutes. It feels like hours.

They could be anywhere by now.

Dry Alpha-Bits from the box. Uses a small rubber spatula to scrape at the insides of the Nutella jar. Pulls the curtain aside and looks out the living room window. The driveway is still empty.

Looooong gooooooone.

She opens her notebook and looks back through her entries under *Rage* to see if he has ever done anything this drastic before. There was the example from November when he was drying dishes during Stage 4 and practically flung the cutlery into the drawer. Including knives! Or that time in January he was shovelling the sidewalk—hacking the shovel's wide blade into the white, scraping it across the pavement and hurling mounds of snow to the side with a grunt. When he finally came inside to track her down, his face was red, beads of sweat dripped from his brow. Luckily, the children were safe in the linen closet.

She tries to imagine what he could be capable of today.

Oh, you have no idea.

Her jaw aches, her body tingles and her face is swollen. Her teeth feel like they're floating. Even her socks are too tight. She loosens her belt and undoes the top button on her jeans. It seems as if she is moving through thick, clear liquid. Like the coupling gel used in an ultrasound. Her head feels carbonated. Picks the last bits of oatmeal from the baking pan with two fingers, licks them, eyes shut. The kids really would have loved this crumble, she thinks. A tear trickles down her cheek and a low hum emerges from her throat.

At least they would have used utensils.

When she can't imagine eating anything else, Karina goes into the bathroom. She locks the door out of habit even though no one's home. She can solve this. She twists the graduation ring her parents bought her off her right hand and places it on her left for safekeeping, above the wedding band. Hitches her hair into a ponytail then puts three fingers to the back of her mouth to trigger her gag reflex. She has no choice. She can do this almost silently, though her eyes tend to get somewhat bloodshot after.

Each release works toward a balancing of the account. A retching reckoning, a history of her loss of control. She continues until the last of the first bite is gone. It doesn't take long to reverse it all and regain her power. Four minutes. Maybe five.

A chunk of pink rhubarb skin and a half dozen Alpha-Bits linger in the bowl after she flushes. She squints for a moment and tries to make words out of the floating letters. *TIP*, *RUIN*, *TRIP*, *TRU*. She wipes the splashes off the seat. *TURNIP*. Flushes again and puts the lid down. She scrubs her hands, switches her ring back, blows her nose, brushes her teeth, wipes the mascara away from under her eyes, lets her hair down, unlocks the door, takes a deep breath and steps back into the kitchen.

Anne can't abide the mess, or the afterburn in the back of Karina's throat. She gives Karina the silent treatment.

There is a newspaper on the kitchen table, where he was sitting during Stage 3. *The Globe and Mail.* She hadn't noticed it before. His glasses are beside it. And a Hello Kitty pencil. The paper is folded open to the crossword puzzle. Half the squares are filled in with his tidy, dark upper case letters. He was doing a crossword puzzle during a Stage 3 Temper Buildup. She makes a note of this discovery in her notebook under the heading *Things He Does to Make Everything Look Normal.*

Then she starts cleaning.

The truck pulls into the driveway as she puts the last dish away and dries her hands on a tea towel. She eyes the cast-iron frying pan.

Now's your chance, whispers Anne, perking up again. *Grab it. Hide behind the door. Quick!*

The girls blast in, windblown, smiling. "Dessert time! Dessert time! Daddy said so. He said woo-bawb cwumble," shouts Nina.

"I hope she never learns to properly pronounce rhubarb," says Tyler. "It cracks me up." He doesn't see Karina, and speaks loudly. "Karina? You home? Hello?"

Hold it up high. Both hands. Bring it down hard.

Karina can practically hear the clang. She imagines the sound, the vibration, warm and deeply satisfying. Like Tibetan singing bowls. With an echo like expectations met.

Tyler is holding something. A plastic Save-On-Foods bag.

"I got us some ice cream!"

Golden opportunity. If you don't do it now, you're on your own. Listen to me, or I swear I'm leaving.

"The fancy kind. Couldn't resist. Häagen-Dazs. French vanilla."

She lowers the frying pan slowly, pushes the door aside and steps forward. She knows Anne doesn't mean it. She knows she'll never leave.

"Bad news," says Karina. "I burned the whole pan. Had to throw it all away. I can whip up another batch, easy."

He wipes a tear away from her cheek, shakes his head, smiles and kisses her like nothing was ever accounted for, like nothing ever happened.

What the Cat Coughed Up

So, my sweet, shall I tell you again? The story of when you were wee? The story of how you came to be here? Yes? All right then my kitty, fold back your ears and enjoy. Don't purr too loud or you'll miss the best parts.

Back when you were just a scruffy little fluffball, black as night and soft as smoke, someone put you in a shoebox and left you on the doorstep of the animal shelter.

The volunteer who discovered you opened the lid of the box, and there you were. The prettiest little kitty cat she'd ever seen. She snapped a photo of you for the shelter's website. The adoption applications poured in.

A young couple—let's call them the Smiths—fit all the required criteria. They were overjoyed to be selected as your new family.

The volunteer warned Mr. and Mrs. Smith of the dangers of coyotes and antifreeze and cheap, grocery-store cat food. You were so cute; she was sad to see you leave the animal shelter parking lot in the Smiths' hybrid car. But she had a job to do, and she took her responsibilities seriously. (You did notice her slip the application fee into her jean jacket pocket, you smart creature. I tell you: it took a mere ten minutes for her to lose it all on the slots at Chances Casino that night.)

At your new home, there was a cat door for easy access to the front garden, a cat tower made of wood and carpet, a fuzzy ball with a tinkly bell inside and a miniature fishing rod with a yellow-dyed feather on the end that Mr. and Mrs.

Smith would tease you with. You made your new owners laugh and laugh. "What a sweet little firecracker you are!" they said. "Who ever said a black cat was bad luck?"

You let them pat you and nuzzle their faces into your soft fur. They poured you cream and watched you lick it up. You kneaded their thighs and found comfort upon their laps. The arrangement suited you just fine.

Then Mrs. Smith's belly grew large.

Mr. Smith would lay his head against it like it was some velvet cushion. He'd stroke the veiny orb and smile like he'd caught a mouse. They no longer dangled the yellow feather from the fishing rod for you. They no longer nuzzled you. Your mustard-yellow eyes narrowed and your whiskers twitched when Mrs. Smith lifted her shirt and gazed at her moon-shaped figure in the full-length mirror. You suspected there was a separate living thing within that huge, grotesque belly.

And since you are a cat, the wisest of creatures, you were correct.

Soon there appeared a small, hairless thing in your home.

The Smiths became obsessed with this shrill and sticky flesh-ball. They rarely let it out of their sight. They held it against their chests and shoulders and tapped its back until it belched or vomited. They collected its feces in soft white cloths. They acted as though the thing was the prince of Persia.

When you wound yourself around their legs in a sultry figure eight, they booted you across the hardwood floor. When you settled upon their laps, you were tossed aside like a snotty wet wipe. They nailed plywood over the cat door and called it babyproofing. They put the cat tower on the back deck to make room for a new changing table.

You were in the crib when the child stopped breathing.

It was only a minute or two, really. The thing was barely even blue when Mr. and Mrs. Smith came into the room, became instantly hysterical and flung you out by the tail. You lay in the hallway half-dazed and humiliated. The paramedics practically trampled you on their way to the nursery.

Everyone blew it all out of proportion. The next day you were thrown into the Prius and driven back to the animal shelter. They told the volunteer that you were wicked; that you had tried to kill their precious child. They accused you of trying to suffocate it. Of drawing its breath away. Of putting a curse on it.

The volunteer was skeptical. She knew what new parents were like.

She clicked her tongue and told them it was way, way, way more difficult to re-home an older cat.

I know, I know! *Older!* You hadn't even had your first birthday. People have a warped sense of the aging process these days. But let's not get sidetracked.

"Well, do what you gotta do," said Mr. Smith.

The volunteer told them there was a return fee.

"No problemo," said Mrs. Smith, and whipped out her debit card.

"Oh. Sorry," said the volunteer. "Our machine thingy's broken. Do you have cash?"

Mr. Smith held the baby while Mrs. Smith dug through her purse. The volunteer started preparing the "Return of Animal" paperwork.

You know a window of opportunity when you see it.

Even if they had put in more of an effort, it's doubtful anyone could have caught you when you bolted. Like a demon on a day pass, you darted across the mini-mall parking lot, along the boulevard, over a six-lane bridge and through the adjacent neighbourhood. You ran through playgrounds, backyards, a cemetery and a minigolf course until you were outside the city limits on a pathway that led into the dark woods.

The sky became black with storm clouds. Rain fell in thick waves. But did that stop you?

No!

It slowed you down somewhat, but you were a trouper. Your tail dragged through mud and puddles. Your whiskers, wilted and sad, stopped functioning properly and you kept bonking into rocks and tree stumps. Your soaked black fur stuck to your pale skin. You looked like a goth girl who'd fallen out of a canoe.

Finally you came to a clearing and through wet yellow eyes you saw the cottage. When you leapt into my arms, you nearly knocked me over. You were so much bigger than the last time I'd seen you!

I set aside the crystal ball through which I'd been watching your journey. I dried your fur with a tea towel and wiped the muck from your paw pads.

But you were not well. You coughed and sputtered. It sounded grave. Others would have blamed the cold wind and rain, but I knew better. You'd fulfilled your purpose, so I gave you a potion that would make you expel the tender inner linings of your lungs.

Others would say you spat up a hairball, but again, I knew better. I picked the inner linings of your lungs off the floor so carefully. They were delicate, like silver doilies, and they contained the molecules of genuine terror that I'd been hoping to acquire for many, many years.

I lay them flat on a cookie sheet and dried them at a controlled temperature in the oven overnight. The next day I crumbled your discarded lung linings between my palms until they formed a coarse dust. There was enough of this powder to fill a medium-sized jam jar, which I labelled *Nightmares of a Human Infant.*

Others would say that infants can't *have* nightmares, for they have yet to experience evil in their short, innocent lives. But I know better. And so did you. Undefined evil, unlabelled fear, unnamed terror is the wickedest kind. And the most potent.

I am so grateful to you for bringing me these nightmares. These gems.

So difficult to obtain! And such an essential ingredient for creating elixirs, potions and poisons. You did a wonderful job, my precious cat.

Now, now. Don't look at me like that. Your lung tissue regenerated in no time, good as new. Come onto my lap. Knead my old thighs as you wish.

And always remember my promise: no more shoeboxes for you.

The Virgin and the Troll

Hyperventilating made the virgin in the prison tower light-headed. Dark blotches flitted across the lids of her eyes when she shut them. Her tongue felt thick, her lips tingled and her fists were clenched so tightly her fingernails dug into the palms of her hands. A bird flew by the high rotunda window, and in her envy and rage the virgin spat at it. This did not help her state of mind. She touched the back of her neck, squeezed the muscles there and considered her impending decapitation. Would it hurt? Where would the pain be felt? A growl in her throat became a wail that was heard throughout the kingdom.

The virgin's father hadn't *meant* for things to end up like this.

Of course he felt terrible.

He had simply been trying to give his only child the life she deserved: a better life than that of a poor carpenter's daughter, one of poverty and hardship. The man knew the girl, who had blossomed like a daisy in a latrine, had no chance to *meet* a rich, handsome man like the king, let alone marry into such privilege.

But... what if?

The father was certain if His Highness felt a wisp of the virgin's silky hair, gazed into her blue eyes, heard her sweet voice and saw the way she swayed her ample hips when she walked, why, he would be unable to resist her charms.

Have not men exaggerated their daughters' better qualities for generations? Put their girls' gifts in the most positive light? Made slightly more of those fine features, generous curves and unique talents than the confines of reality would permit? So he'd told one little fib... How was the man to know the king would take him at his word?

It had been the father's carpentry skills that first brought him within the royal court's walls to fix a broken spindle on a royal staircase. The king, bored, struck up a conversation with the tradesman. They spoke of the changing weather, the problem of too much mead before midday and whether young people these days spent too much time playing card games. Eventually the king inquired after the carpenter's own family. "My wife died many years ago," the father said. "During childbirth. Her legacy—my daughter—is one in a million."

"One in a million, you say?" The king nodded to his chamberlain, who stood at the ruler's side, holding a stein of dark ale and an oily roast mutton sandwich on a silver tray. "Carpenter claims his daughter is 'one in a million.' How many times have we heard that?"

"Perhaps a million times, Your Highness," said the king's right-hand man, who seemed to grin and purse his lips simultaneously.

"Indeed! And now, a million and one!" They both chortled, then the king took a quaff of ale.

Nonetheless, the man felt he had his lowly foot in the royal door. "If you permit, Your Highness," he said, fumbling with his tool belt, "truly, it is so. My daughter is verily fair. Eyes of blue and hair of gold. Indeed, she would please you well."

"Ah, beautiful women are as common as crabapples," scoffed the king, reaching for the meat sandwich. "She is not special." The chamberlain made a little puffing sound while half closing his eyes.

"But my daughter has breasts like drifts of snow over two round boulders."

"Beautiful breasts are as common as mongrel dogs in the servant quarters," scoffed the king. "Who needs more breasts, eh, man?"

"Who indeed?" said the chamberlain placing his free hand upon his own chest and squeezing gently in the area of the nipple.

The king nodded to his manservant, took another swig of ale and spun on his heel to leave. The opportunity for the virgin to meet the king perched like a flake of snow in the father's dirty, calloused hands. He knew it would melt away forever if he didn't act.

"Wait!" he said without forethought. "Upon my very honour, my daughter *is* one in a million. Why, she… she can turn straw into gold."

The king stopped, wiped the foam and a spot of mustard from his moustache with a royal napkin proffered by the chamberlain, and turned back to the man.

"Straw into gold, you say?"

"That's right. She, uh, does this with only a spinning wheel and a reel, Your Highness." The father's mind was on fire.

"I see," said the king. "Have we ever seen such a talent?" he asked his chamberlain.

"Indeed, we have not."

The king stared into the middle distance.

"Your Highness?" whispered the chamberlain.

The king did not answer. He was in a daze. Although he lived a pampered life—his daily expenses covered by taxes collected from peasants and gentry—there was never enough wealth to fulfill the king's secret wish: to host a spectacular outdoor music festival on his land and invite the entire kingdom. If this carpenter's claims were true, the girl's unique talent would surely finance such an event! He would hire the finest musicians in all the land. Elevated platforms would be erected throughout the property, so the performers would be safe from the rabble, yet the rabble could see and hear the performers. People would dress in extravagant costumery for the occasion. Feathers. Furs. Masks and lace. People from far and wide would frolic for three, possibly four days straight. Singing, dancing, rounds and reels. Leaping and tumbling together.

"Your Highness? Your Highness? Is all well?"

The king blinked several times and cleared his throat. "Yes. Indeed. Quite well." He regarded the carpenter. "Gold spinning you say? That is an art that pleases me. If your daughter is as clever as you say, bring her to my palace in the morrow and I will put her to the test."

The king's chamberlain contacted the local Waldorf school, which supplied him with a spinning wheel and a reel, then called in a favour from a farmer friend up the valley and had a large quantity of straw delivered.

Now the father sat at the base of the rotunda in which his daughter was imprisoned, listening to her howl and cry from the tiny window at the top. Each wet sniff, each fretful moan a dagger in his heart. He smacked the back of his head against the customized slate, a feeble attempt to transfer the pain of sorrow and regret in his heart into his own skull; for alas, there was no one to blame for the virgin's imprisonment but himself.

In time, there was a lull in his daughter's cries. "Darling?" he called up to her, thinking to bring her a measure of relief. "Sweetheart! It is I, your father!"

"Dad? Is that you down there?"

He jumped to his feet and reached toward the voice. But even with arms stretched high above, it was still a good three cubits to the bottom ledge of the tiny window.

"Yes! Dear child, take comfort knowing that your father and protector is nearby."

There was some shuffling from above. A grunt. Suddenly, a cascade of straw landed upon the man's head.

He picked the bits of the dry barnyard bedding from his hair and face, spat out that which had gone into his mouth and brushed it from his shoulders.

"You are in distress, it is clear," he called, while shaking smaller bits from inside the back of his shirt. "I understand. But never fear. I shall save you, dear daughter. I shall..."

"Go away, asshole!" she cried. "Haven't you done enough damage for one day?" Then the virgin dropped another armful of straw upon her father's head—followed by her shoe, which was fashioned from wood and leather with a metal clasp at the toe.

When he had made the claim, the father was quite confident his daughter wouldn't need to actually spin anything into anything. He figured the king would clap eyes upon her, fall crown over slippers in love and forget about spindles, trundle pedals and the accumulation of yet more gold. Therefore, he did not inform the virgin of this fabrication. Why bother? That night, while supping on watery leek and potato soup, he simply let her know he had arranged for her to have an audience with the handsome king.

"You *what?* You're setting me up?"

"A simple 'Thank you, Father' would suffice," said the father.

"So now I'm just a piece of meat?"

"Not just any meat, my dear. Fine marbled ribeye."

"Wow. You are a creep." The virgin picked up her bowl, drank the last of the broth with a slurp, slammed it down and stomped across the room to the other side of the cottage.

There had been a time when the girl had looked upon her father as if he were a god. As if he could do no wrong. But now? She looked at him askance across the breakfast table. She did not seek his advice over dinner. And she no longer wished to sit with him at the end of the day, watching the candle burn down. Did she not realize his genuine desire to capitalize on her beauty and virtue? To afford them both a life of luxury, of velvet leggings as daywear, chairs so soft two servants are required to help lift a person out, and cheese-cake with tea every afternoon?

Eventually the virgin came to see the wisdom in her father's proposal. "Fine," she said. "As long as you won't be there breathing down my neck." The man was delighted. "And I'll have you know that soon as I've had a good look around the castle, I'm outta there."

The father instructed her on using enough—but not too much—blusher from ground, dried berries for her lips and fair cheeks and charcoal around her eyes. He insisted she wear the dress his wife had worn on their wedding night. It was a bit tight and the girl fairly burst out of it in the front. She protested, but the man assured her such was the style royal gentlemen preferred.

In a tin box hidden under the man's bed lay the only two remaining items by which the man could remember his wife: the tarnished stick barrette she'd worn in her hair and a charm bracelet that had adorned her delicate wrist. Gently, the man handed them to his daughter for the occasion.

"Wear these, dear daughter, in good faith," he said.

She scowled and held them before her face, examining them as if she were sizing up a couple of brown trout from the fishmonger at the local market.

"I thought you'd hawked these," said the girl with a sneer.

It came as no surprise to the man that fifteen was the average age at which spirited virgins were traditionally married off by their fathers, who sought to restore peace and order to the family home. He could understand the rationale.

She put the accessories on nevertheless, and the man's heart tightened as he noticed how she resembled her mother. He touched the girl's shoulder tenderly, then recomposed himself.

"Now then. Give the king a lick," he advised, "but not a bite. Though of royal blood, he is but a man. Let him peruse your wares with his royal gaze, but do not allow him to sample the merchandise. Not yet." The girl rolled her lined eyes as girls oftentimes do. They sat on the stoop of their tiny cottage, the girl as far away from her father as was possible without falling into the potato patch, and awaited the arrival of the king's coach.

Outside the royal mansion the father was surrounded by the straw his daughter had dumped upon him. He picked up a piece and rolled it between his fingers, wondering how indeed the rough grass, the bedding of gardens, the fibre of nests, could be transformed into fine gold. The hard end of the straw was handy for picking bits of the previous day's meal from the wide gaps between the man's teeth. Although not a religious man, he pressed his hands together, the straw pressed between his palms, and prayed. He repented to God for some old sins and begged for magic power to take hold of his daughter so she could know the specific alchemy for the task required of her. It was the only way for her to save herself, and finally bring him the honour and respect he deserved.

Surely the king wouldn't *literally* have her head if she could not fulfill what he had so offhandedly promised. Surely the king was exaggerating.

The virgin's cries of sorrow changed to shouts of fury, and with each poisonous cuss, the furrow in his heart deepened. Would the anguish of a father whose good intentions backfired ever end?

A sudden rustling in a nearby juniper bush startled him. He drew in his breath and remained still until—was it a stag? a small bear?—a stunted man leapt from the greenery! A single brow stretched wildly above bulging eyes. His nose looked like a misshapen root vegetable, the kind that would be sold at a discounted price at the market at closing time. Curly hairs not unlike those in a man's dark areas protruded from his collar, around his wrists and from a crude gap between the top of his unbelted trousers and a ragged vest that spoke of another era.

The troll stood for a moment regarding the man, then cocked his head skyward and grinned at the high-pitched vulgarities streaming from the tiny window above them.

"Hey, ho!" said the dwarfish stranger. "Sounds like someone's moon-time." His voice was like the scraping of a shovel against a rock. The father was too shocked to respond.

"I say, is that the wench's shoe?" the little fellow said.

"Y-y-yes. Er, indeed, it belongs to my daughter."

"A daughter? I like daughters. Do tell."

And with the mention of her, the man's grief erupted once again. It could not be helped. The unhappy saga was recounted to the manikin, who listened with great interest.

"Boost me up then," he said when the father had finished.

"Prithee, pardon?"

"Boost me up, sir. I can help."

The troll claimed to possess the very powers the man had been praying for. So the father hoisted him up over his head. He was the size of a small sled dog, but muscular and strong. He wobbled a bit and nearly fell, but finally managed to grab the iron bars and lift himself to the tower window.

The king and his chamberlain had begun planning the music festival as soon as the carpenter took leave. They brainstormed which troubadours would be summoned and considered when best to have heralds announce the event.

"Since some people will be in fancy costume," said the king, "I think a band round the wrist of festival merrymakers would help us identify participants."

"We'll call it a wristband!" said the chamberlain.

"Yes! And each of these wristbands shall be of a different hue. For royalty, purple of course. Nobility, blue. And peasants? They can have brown wristbands. Of course, there will be barons who wish to rondeau with commoners' daughters and sisters, and in my festival they shall be able to do so freely. But if the viceroy of North Vancouver is going to dance a quadrille, shouldn't he at least know it is with a common gong farmer's daughter?" They both laughed at the visual.

"And if it rains?" said the chamberlain. "Would you consider moving the festival indoors?"

"Oh, you are a negative Nelly," said the king, touching the chamberlain on his cheek. "It wouldn't dare rain. But if it does, it will be all the more memorable as men and women, young and old, dance in clothing so wet it sticks to their bodies." Together they sat in silent reverie picturing the scene in their heads, until the chamberlain broke the spell: "And if the wench is unable to produce the gold?"

The king sighed. "Well, Mr. Goblet-Half-Empty, I suppose then we'll have to just give up my lifelong dream and subsist on the taxpayers' meagre payments and love."

Of course, the father had hitched a ride with a passerby and followed the king's coach when it arrived to gather the girl from their cottage. Perhaps the father of a dozen daughters would simply let one of them go off to meet a man with nothing more than a kiss on her forehead and a pat on her padded rump. But not this father. With his carpenter's belt slung around his waist, he had slipped through the gate and across the drawbridge unquestioned. He was in the king's drawing room, making as if to fix a squeaky door on a cabinet when he heard the virgin, and presumably the coachman, enter the Great Hall.

He hid when he saw them.

"Holy shit," the virgin exclaimed. "Quite the lobby." The man nearly bit his own tongue clear off to prevent himself from shouting, "Be not so impressed that you appear wanting!"

"Wait here," said a voice. Footsteps echoed. A door. Another door. More footsteps.

"Good day, mistress." There could be no mistaking the king himself. The father wondered how it was that even the man's voice sounded prosperous? The way he lingered on his vowels made his words positively drip with wealth and grandeur. The father made a vow to emulate this lingering of vowels in his own speech from then on.

"Good day, Your Highness," replied the virgin. The man imagined his dear daughter curtsying. He was beaming.

"Your father speaks highly of you," said the king.

Silence.

Good girl, thought the man. Let him see for himself. Let him take the time to assess your virtues, up and down.

"He is a fine carpenter, your father. In fact, he crafted this very table."

There was much rapping of knuckles upon wood, mumbling agreements and praise. The man's craftsmanship had always been a point of pride, even if the trade did not provide his small family with the wealth to which he aspired.

The king cleared his throat. "So, I hear you can spin straw into gold."

Oh, blasphemy! thought the man. *Please dear child, bend over a little. Flutter your eyelashes! Let down your hair! Do what you must to distract him!*

"Um, hang on. I can what?"

"Spin straw into gold. With nothing more than a spinning wheel and a reel." A pause. "Eh, man? Am I right?"

"Bang on, Your Highness," said the chamberlain.

"Who told you that?"

"Your father. He boasted of it. That is why I have brought you here."

"Okay. Wait a sec," she said. "My dad told you that I could spin straw? Into *fucking gold?* I can't even sew a button onto a burlap sack."

"Enough!" bellowed the king. "You will spin the straw into gold by morn, or I'll have your head."

In the drawing room the father held his breath and squeezed his eyes shut and wished with all his might for the side of the mountain above them to collapse and send a torrent of mud, rock and debris into the valley, flooding the township and wiping the castle from the face of the earth along the way.

But of course the mountain had not collapsed, and the father found himself hoisting a dwarf up the rotunda wall to the window of his daughter's prison cell. The little man must have surprised the virgin; a high-pitched scream was followed by the yelp of the manikin and the *thwack-oomph-thwack* of the girl trying to push the intruder back out the window.

But the fellow was tough and ornery. His kicking feet eventually disappeared between the window bars and into the tower cell. There was more hitting, more screaming and cussing. The man could hear the troll's sandpapery voice beg the girl for calm.

In time, the ruckus subsided, and the voices dropped low. The two seemed to be discussing something. The father heard snippets: "Over my dead body," and "I'd like to see you try," and "Not bad for a punk." And then there was a buzzing. No, a whirring. It sounded like a spinning wheel.

What the father didn't hear, once his daughter settled down, were her *ooh*s and *aah*s of amazement. She sat cross-legged on the rotunda floor, resting her elbows upon her knees and her chin in her hands, watching the visitor's stubby fingers pull handfuls of straw roving, his little legs pump the treadle, the flyer and the bobbin fire round, and a stream of gold leap off the wheel like flames off a dry log.

"You're so graceful," said the girl. No one had ever called the troll graceful before, and he blushed. "I can't believe it's really gold. You must be the richest guy alive," she said.

"Nah. I used to be rich. Nothing but trouble. I found it too difficult to tell who my real friends were. So I rarely do this anymore. People get funny when they find out you can turn stuff into gold."

"Of course they do," said the girl. "It *is* funny." The dwarf stopped for a moment, and looked up at the girl. "You've got to admit. It's hilarious. I mean, it's like you're eating ice cubes and shitting diamonds."

"Yes. Now that you put it that way, I suppose it is!"

"It's just another weird thing the body can do."

The two spoke of party tricks and unusual talents. She pulled her hair away from her face and moved one eye around in a circle as if it were the blade of a windmill, while the other gazed straight ahead. He stood transfixed. Then she belched the first few measures of a Gallican plainsong. He smiled and shook his head in disbelief. She showed him how she could blow bubbles out of saliva and flick them off the end of her curled tongue. He laughed so hard he nearly caught his beard in the whorl.

"The human body is truly a miracle," he said once he caught his breath. "Yours brings me such joy."

The girl smiled. "And yours has saved my life."

Eventually, the father spied the dwarf's feet swinging out of the window.

"Help me down, kind sir," he cried, and the carpenter let him stand on his shoulders to descend the rotunda wall.

The hairy fellow had a satisfied look upon his face, which the father did not trust.

"You were right," said the little man, leering. "She's useless on the spinning wheel. But I did the work for her, and she repaid me in kind."

He winked.

The father knew that more had happened in the tower than simply spinning, and he lunged for the troll, his fists at the ready. *Has he defiled my princess?* He swung like a mad rooster. But as the troll ducked and wove, something sparkled in his forelock.

The man stopped.

Could it be? Yes! The barrette! His beloved wife's heirloom!

The father snorted through his nose like an angry grizzly. Although the meanderings of his imagination caused him great distress, he knew that in spinning the straw into gold, the runt had done a service that may have secured the virgin's chance of the king giving her his attention. How could he resent that the girl gave him her mother's hair accessory? Better that than her honour.

He owed the vile fellow an apology. He took a deep breath. "Excuse my outburst. In truth, man, I am grateful to you. And I don't even know your name!"

The manikin told him to think no more of it, then introduced himself. But in the next instant he snatched the virgin's shoe off the ground, held it to his face, inhaled lustily, then dashed into the forest with it, leaving the man standing in a pile of hay, boiling mad, the runt's name already forgotten.

The father passed a long and fitful night but despite the crick in his neck from sleeping sitting up, he awoke hopeful. Certainly the king would enter the cell soon, see the pile of gold, a royal engagement would be announced and the village's finest wedding planners would be summoned. The man assumed there would be a decree that, as the king's royal father-in-law, he would be assigned a chamberlain of his own. His beard would be trimmed by the royal barber. His bunions would be treated by the royal podiatrist.

He heard a door open from the tower above.

"Your Highness." His daughter's voice was groggy, as if she had slept poorly. At least she was being polite, thought the man, quietly congratulating himself on raising a daughter who minded her manners. "Here's your spun gold."

The king didn't immediately answer. The father imagined him running his wealthy fingers through the gilded treasure.

He hoped his daughter's charcoaled eyes remained fresh and her dress was unwrinkled.

"Impressive," the king finally said. The man sighed in relief.

"Okay. So put a fork in me. I'm done here."

Oh, dear girl, this would be far easier if you restrained your sharp tongue, the man despaired.

The king chuckled. "Not quite. Guards!"

There was a rush of stomping feet, followed by the roll of… a trolley? A cart? Wheelbarrow?

"Dump it there, men," commanded the king.

"Jesus! More straw?" the man heard his daughter say. "You've got to be kidding me."

"Do I jest, man?" the king said.

"No, Your Highness." It was the voice of the chamberlain. "Just the jester jests."

"Witty," said the king. "Now. This time—ten sheaths! You will spin this straw into gold by tomorrow morn, or I'll have your head."

And with that, there were more footsteps, the chortling of men, the slamming of a door and the turning of a lock.

This time, instead of wet weeping and fretful moaning, it was a torrent of blasphemies and pirate-speak that sent a dagger through the man's heart. Again: *smack*, *smack*, *smack* went his head against the slate wall, until he could no longer remain silent: "Daughter! Dear daughter! I am here, your father and protector. Have faith! No harm shall come to you."

Down came more straw, followed by the contents of her chamber pot. "Screw you," she said. As he wiped his hair and face dry with the tail of his shirt, her other shoe clipped him upon his right ear.

Suddenly, the little troll reappeared. He was still wearing the barrette, though it was so tangled in the coarse black hair it was barely visible.

He stood for a moment, regarding the father, cocked his head and grinned as the high-pitched vulgarities streamed from the tiny window above them.

"She's a feisty lass, she is," he said. His voice made the father's skin feel as if covered in rash.

"Well? Can you help?" asked the man, plumbing his throat for a polite voice.

"At your service," replied the hairy wart. "Boost me up!" And with that, he leapt toward the man, who had no choice but to catch him in his arms and lift him overhead. This time, the girl reached out eagerly for the dwarf's thick paws and helped him climb over the sill and through the window. The father heard not screaming this time, but ebullient chatter from the tower cell. He thought he heard snippets of "Hey, no peeking," and "Don't be silly, you're just the perfect height," and "Maybe one day I could teach you!" Then came more shuffling about, some laughter and finally, spinning.

What the father didn't hear was the manikin ask the virgin if she'd ever seen the ocean. Of course, being cloistered *and* poor, she had not, so as he was spinning, he spoke to her of salty waves that pulsed upon the sandy shore like the rhythm of blood in and out of the heart's chambers. He told her of whirlpools and eddies, tiny universes that feasted upon boulders until they were grains of sand. He told her of the early morning sea mist that rose like steam from God's kettle and tasted like tears.

"Ah, you are my poet," said the girl dreamily.

"And you are my muse," replied the troll.

"I don't know what a muse is, but if it means someone who can blow bubbles off her tongue, then yes, I'm your muse."

"You, my darling, are one in a million," he said, and promised that one day he'd take her to the ocean and they'd dunk their faces into the water and he'd teach her to blow bubbles through her nose.

"Oh, hey! That reminds me," said the girl, hopping to her feet. "Check this out." She picked up one of the thinner strands of gold and poked it up her nose, snorted a few times, coughed, kept wiggling, snorting and pushing until the strand appeared at the back of her throat, between her tonsils. She coughed again, gagged a little, then reached her hand into her mouth.

"Taa-daa!" said the girl, slowly pulling the gold all the way through and holding the wet filament in front of her smiling face.

The dwarf clapped his hands. "I think I'm in love."

By the time the little man's feet reappeared through the tower window, the father's pacing had worn the manicured lawn beside the wall to a dirt path.

"Help me down, sir!" the troll cried, and the man guided the piggish feet onto his shoulders so he could descend.

The troll bore a joyful, easy look, which troubled the man greatly.

"Wow," said the troll. "She may be useless on the spinning wheel, but the girl's got other talents." He licked his lips.

Again, the man seethed at the things he imagined until he could bear it no longer. He made for the manikin's throat, nostrils flared, vision blurry with hot hatred. The dwarf grabbed his wrists and held him back. "Hey, ho! She repaid me fairly and honourably." The man saw the charm bracelet wrapped around the dwarf's thick forearm. He knew that the troll had provided a service that may have saved his daughter's life. He could not begrudge him the bracelet.

The father took a deep breath and said painfully, "I will admit that you are indeed a hero, Master…?"

The troll relaxed his grip and said "The name's…" but as he spoke, he eyed the virgin's other shoe, lying on the ground. It was all the man could do not to roar in anger when the hideous creature picked up the shoe, rubbed the sole of it across his chest as if it were a cake of soap, then dashed into the forest.

The father passed another long and fitful night leaning against the rotunda wall. But despite the insect bites on his face and hands and the dried urine stiffening his hair, he awakened hopeful. He was certain the king would soon enter the tower cell, see the pile of gold, and a wedding would be announced that very day. Royal chefs would begin menu planning. The royal tailor would take his measurements.

A door opened. Footsteps.

"Your Highness," said the virgin. The man was pleased that she addressed the king with honour. He hoped some water had been provided, with which his daughter might freshen herself. He hoped there was a looking glass in the tower cell, into which she could gaze as she adjusted her hair and flattened her eyebrows.

"You have proven yourself," said the king, his royal voice clearly audible through the window. The man sighed in relief. He could almost hear the sound of trumpets heralding joyful news of upcoming nuptials.

"Great. Now, let me out of here, dickhead."

Oh, dear God in heaven, is there any creature on this earth with greater swings of mood than a woman of fifteen?

"You humour me, wench," said the king patiently. "Does she humour you, too?"

"A regular travelling circus act she is, Your Highness," said the chamberlain.

"There is one more test. Guards!"

Again, there was the stomping of feet, followed by the roll of what sounded like a heavy cart. Or two.

"Shovel it out there, men," commanded the king.

"Oh. My. God. Are you frigging nuts?" said the girl.

"Why, you petulant little..." It was the chamberlain. It seemed he had lost patience with the virgin.

"Stop, man," commanded the king. And in a hushed tone, but not so hushed that the father could not hear, he said, "Don't let our pimply wench irritate you. Remember, without her there is no music. No merry dancing. No gay festival."

There was an audible sigh, presumably from the manservant.

"By the way, what do you think of this: 'The King and His Chamberlain's Festival of Song and Dance'?"

"Forsooth?" The chamberlain perked up.

"Catchy, is it not? I can almost hear the fiddle, dulcimer, clavichord and transverse flute now."

The man below did not see the chamberlain making tiny fluttering claps with the tips of his fingers. He was unaware of the chamberlain's feet as they danced in quick double-steps and delicate bransle singles, or the upturned corners of his lips when the king whispered the words "Trust me" to him before turning back to the girl.

But he did hear a distinct lowering of the king's voice when he said, "Fifty sheaths. Spin all this straw into gold by tomorrow morn, and in return, I shall marry you and make you my queen."

Down below, the father very nearly burst. Vindicated! After all his sacrifices, worry and woe, the virgin was to marry the man who could finally give her the life she deserved.

"Daughter! Dear daughter!" the man cried up to the window once he heard the king and his men depart. "You are to become queen, my sweet. Did I not tell you it would all work out? Did I not tell you the king would be unable to resist your charms? Did I not predict tha..."

A gob of warm saliva landed upon the man's head and dribbled onto the bridge of his nose. He recalled that young virgins may suffer from anxiety prior to their weddings, and figured this must be the case. He knew he must don a maternal apron to guide her through her premarital jitters.

"I realize the pending nuptials make you feel uneasy," he said. "Nervous. This is natural, my darling. Women have always..."

"Shut *up!*" the girl screamed, and proceeded to call her father an effing this and an effing that, until he gave up trying to reason with her, slumped down with his fingers in his ears and his eyelids squeezed shut and hoped that the king would not hear the unladylike words spewing from his practically betrothed's lips and change his royal mind.

The virgin was still shrieking when the manikin tapped the father upon his shoulder. He was wearing the barrette and charm bracelet. The man was glad to see the crude and ugly troll, for he knew this was the last time his spinning services would be required. The troll stood for a moment, hairy, muscular arms crossed over his chest. The virgin must have seen him from the tower window, for her voice abruptly changed and she sang out, sweetly as a songbird, "Yooooo-hooooooo, I'm reaaaaaaaaady."

The runt smiled crookedly at the man. "Boost me up, Daddy-O."

It crossed the man's mind that his daughter possessed no other jewellery to give. She'd already bestowed upon him the only two items of value that she had. He feared the greedy dwarf would take that which had been promised to another if she had no treasures left to give.

"Listen, friend," the father said. "Before I do so, I must express my gratitude. Your help has been deeply appreciated. And you have been rewarded generously with a barrette and a charm bracelet. We are a poor family. Those are the only valuables we have. My daughter has nothing more to give you now."

"Ah, your daughter's trinkets are not what I desire."

The man decided to appeal to the dwarf's natural paternal sensibilities. He lowered his voice to be sure the girl would not hear. "Kind sir. I beseech you, man to, uh, man: leave my daughter's honour intact, for she has been bequeathed to another. She is to marry the king anon." The troll shifted his weight from side to side and tapped his stubby foot. "However, to, uh, show our gratitude for your service, if you help her spin the last of the straw into gold on this day, I promise that you may have the first child she bears, to raise as your very own. My first grandchild. All yours." As the words passed his lips he wondered if this offer might be ill-considered. But he brushed off the notion like a fly from his face.

"Well, you are quite the loving father," said the hairy rat. "And I hope I shall be one as well, someday."

"Then it is agreed upon," said the man, and extended his hand.

"Agreed," said the manikin. "Her first child will be mine." He clasped the man's hand firmly. "But, first..." said the dwarf. "Do you have your daughter's certificate of birth?"

Indeed, the man did not. "Do I need such a document?"

"Why yes, of course sir! You'll need to procure her certificate of birth before a royal marriage can take place."

"But how do I...? Where would I...?"

"Boost me up, man, and while I do my business with the straw, you go fetch her certificate of birth from the village office. Be quick! It is government run. They close for dinner at high noon."

And with that, the man helped the troll up the side of the rotunda to the window. The girl reached down for him with both hands, and lifted him to her. There was some shuffling about, quiet voices, a bit of giggling, snippets of "Don't ever shave," and "Do that thing with your elbows again!" and "Tell me more about all those waves."

Then, nothing.

The father took a step forward. He touched the slate wall with his fingertips and looked up at the window one last time. He listened for the spinning wheel to begin its lovely whirr. He waited another moment. Nothing yet, but he knew he had to go before the government office closed. What choice did he have but trust the hideous dwarf would keep his promise?

The first thing the father noticed when he returned that afternoon was the straw—must have been fifty sheaths!—on the ground below the rotunda's tiny window. Piled high, and soft enough to cushion a fall, or a jump.

The second thing he noticed were the bars. The two middle ones were bent apart into a diamond shape, wide enough for a troll the size of a sled dog, a woman the size of a small queen and a spinning wheel to squeeze through. Standing at the window was the king, crown in his hand. His head rested upon the chamberlain's shoulder and the chamberlain stroked his employer's royal hair.

The third thing he noticed were the guards. Dozens of them, circling the grounds, as if on the hunt for something. Or someone. He tucked himself into the hollow of a cedar tree until it was safe for him to flee.

And for the next twenty years—or has it been twenty-one?—the father has wandered the land from the soggy southwest coast to the dry hills in the north and the green forests of the east, searching for... who? Was it Shortribs? Sheepshanks? Laceleg? For the very life of him he can't recall the vile troll's name. He isn't sure if he ever knew it at all. Perhaps it doesn't matter. What he does know is that he cannot go home, for the king, whose festival of song and dance is still but a dream, would surely have his head.

So, ever does he search for the nameless dwarf who stole his daughter's heart—and took the rest of her along with it.

Ham

While his two lazy, good-for-nothing brothers sobbed like spoiled toddlers over the loss of their dumpy and (surprise, surprise) uninsured homes, Ham inhaled the pungent fumes that wafted from the burbling cast-iron pot of wolf, twirled around the kitchen/living room of his sturdy little brick house and was overcome by a flash of inspiration that both economists and chefs later called visionary.

"Move it," he said to his oldest brother, Hock, who lay in the fetal position in front of the fridge. "I need to get in there."

Ham grabbed some carrots, celery, onion, half a cob of corn, a fennel bulb and a few other things from the produce drawer. He kicked the fridge door shut, stepped over his sad sack of a sibling and tossed the veggies into the pot, along with some garlic, paprika, salt, pepper and a dash of Frank's Red Hot. Weiner, the middle brother, sniffed, then ate a wayward beet that had fallen onto the floor.

The *Canis lupus* carcass simmered with the extra ingredients in the massive pot in the fireplace for almost two hours. Ham stirred occasionally, added a little of this and a little of that, and finally dipped his ladle in for a sample. Tiny ripples passed along the surface of the broth when he blew on it to cool it down. Then he closed his eyes, reached out his pale-pink lips and slurped. It tasted woodsy. Rich. Like blood and mushrooms. He squealed with delight.

In the time it took for Farmdale municipal police officers to finally arrive and record the brothers' incident statements,

Ham had conceptualized a line of high-end, easy-to-prepare, wolf-broth-based organic meals. He knew he had a winner.

His older brothers eventually waddled off to collect what hadn't been looted from the debris of their blown-down shacks, and figure out what they were going to do with their happily-ever-afters. Ham already knew what he was going to do with his. He drafted a business plan. He tinkered with names, packaging and logo ideas. He calculated his costs and estimated his profits.

"It's a niche market, ripe for exploitation," he said to the branch manager at Farmdale Credit Union. "This soup's time has come." Ham had a reputation as a hard-working perfectionist and the credit union had been tasked with financing local start-ups. Business loans were approved. A line of credit was established. Ham even qualified for the federal government's Rural Entrepreneurs Funding Assistance program.

He wasted no time and hired the best people to develop and refine recipes based on his unique wolf stock. He headhunted talent from Happy Planet. He didn't stop at soup. Stews, curries, marinades and a line of pasta sauces were run through the test kitchen. Focus groups were convened. Target markets were identified. He stacked the organization with young, healthy staff. He knew his brothers were looking for jobs, but he told human resources to give them the runaround. He figured they'd soon give up, and he was right.

At first, Chinny-Chin-Chin Organics was solely available in health food and specialty stores, where the products flew off the shelves. Within sixteen weeks of launching, Sobeys, Nestors and Loblaws picked it up too. The company had to move to a larger manufacturing plant in Richmond. A deal was signed to serve Chinny-Chin-Chin entrees on all Air Canada's long-haul flights. In order to capitalize on the "ethical" market, a portion of the company's profits was donated to Elbows Off the Table, a campaign to promote table manners among underprivileged inner-city kids. Soon, Ham's line competed with Newman's Own for brand recognition and goodwill.

The company's website featured testimonials from people who loved that wolf was a low-cholesterol protein unriddled with antibiotics or artificial hormones. Some gushed about the fairy-tale origins of the company, the rags-to-riches theme on the "About Our Founder" page, and about saying no to victim mentality. There was also an underlying sense that people were enjoying a bit of Old Testament–style vengeance. Wolves had terrorized babies, sheep, pigs and grandmothers for centuries; eating gourmet wolf-based products felt like karma.

And besides, it was delicious.

Taste Magazine called Big Bad Ragu a "shockingly smooth, meaty sauce bursting with hints of pine bark and cedar chips." *Foodies* said, "a splash of Pinot Noir in Forest Chili adds both brightness and acidity, balancing the dense, hearty flavours." *Your Plate or Mine* said, "Our experienced taste-testers couldn't believe this came from a jar!"

Ham became filthy rich. He had a tinge of guilt over having such good fortune while his brothers still struggled to make ends meet. So he sent a few boxes of Sweet-and-Sour Spaghetti Sauce to Weiner and Hock's trailer in Pitt Meadows. Then he blocked their phone numbers and moved to a mansion in West Vancouver. It was built of stainless steel, concrete and live-edged ancient cedar and overlooked Howe Sound. A glass garage door led from the kitchen to the pool area. *Western Living* did a photo shoot for their annual "Who Lives There?" edition.

Life was good.

One morning, he was soaking in his Balinese-inspired hot tub thinking about opportunities in the fast food stream when Karl, Chinny-Chin-Chin's director of corporate communications, phoned. Turns out, some consumer in Ontario had found a strange lump in her Lupus Minestrone.

"So what?" Ham snorted into his wireless iPhone headset. As company president, there were always small fires to put out: copyright issues, product inconsistencies, labour unrest, that kind of thing. He didn't think this was a big deal. Nonetheless, he turned off the hot tub jets so he could concentrate.

Karl's voice cracked a bit. "Well, it was a rather hard lump."

"Who cares? It's not like it's Cream of Wolf soup, where everything gets whipped together. It's minestrone! There's chunks!"

"Sir, it was a tooth."

What did she expect to find? A pearl earring? "Write a cheque to shut her up," snorted Ham. "Talk to Legal."

But it wasn't as easy as that.

Turns out the woman had thought the lump in question was a garbanzo bean or a bit of raw carrot and swallowed it. It became lodged in her esophagus and she was rushed to the hospital in Hamilton where minor surgery was required to remove the piece.

"It gets worse," said Karl. "The tooth she swallowed? It was a baby tooth. A teeny tiny wolf fang. So now they're accusing us of killing baby wolves for Chinny-Chin-Chin products."

The company did in fact use baby wolves in the soup. In all their products. It made economic sense. The less time an animal spent in the breeding facility, the cheaper. Raising wolves to maturity would cut into profit margins. Also, aged wolves had a somewhat rancid flavour compared to the fresher units, kind of like the difference between mutton and lamb. A small population of full-grown wolves was maintained at the facility for breeding purposes. Obviously.

"PETA's up in arms," said Karl. "The SPCA says they're gonna take us to court."

"*People.* They're such hypocrites," said Ham. He got out of the hot tub and put on his navy and burgundy striped velour bathrobe. "You're afraid of a few animal parts in your soup? Here's a thought: stay away from animal soup! The only difference between a wolflet and a full-grown wolf is that the little one's meat is more tender. And they have fewer memories." He paced the length of the pool deck. "Have those bleeding hearts never eaten veal? Do their Beemers not all have soft leather seats? Are they all fucking Buddhists?"

"Actually, uh, they're called pups?" said Karl. "Not wolflets."

"Jesus Christ, Karl, I *know* what baby wolves are called," squealed Ham.

"Yes, sir," said Karl.

The two discussed releasing a proactive statement to the press, a memo to shareholders, a recall of all Lupus Minestrone (or at least a certain batch) and a promise to review their Humane Practices Code. Karl was to issue an immediate order to all employees not to speak to the press, and to draft a Humane Practices Code. Next week they'd look for a ten-kilometre charity run or a writers' festival to sponsor, but for now, staff at both the main Chinny-Chin-Chin production facilities, at the breeding outlet and at head office were told to put their phones straight to voicemail, set an auto-response on their emails and enjoy a complimentary screening of the film *Babe* in the Corporate Entertainment Lounge. Free snacks and drinks were provided.

But social media had already caught wind of the story. Facebook, Twitter and Instagram were abuzz with footage, clearly filmed on the phone of a traitorous employee, of two adorable wolf pups being taken from their howling mother in the breeding facility and brought through the wolf recreation pen (yes, green space for the full-growns) to the rendering plant. The wolf pups had big floppy paws, short snouts and foggy blue eyes. You could practically smell daisies on their breath; they were that goddamn cute.

Not cute was the picture of the Ontario woman who triggered this whole mess lying in her hospital bed looking pathetic, holding the tiny wolf tooth between her fingers. She was surrounded by flowers and stuffed animals and get-well cards. The picture had been "liked" and retweeted by thousands of Canadians (#tinyfanginmysoup #sogross #boycottchin). A GoFundMe page had raised over twenty-four hundred dollars in three hours to help cover therapy for her PTSD.

By 2:20 p.m., a crowd had gathered outside Ham's West Vancouver mansion. He peeked through a crack between the curtains of his library/den at a crowd of people holding hand-drawn placards that read *Howl for Justice!* and *Wee Wee Wee All the Way to Jail*. They were chanting "Chinny-Chin-Chin! In the bin!" There was a Global News van parked in his neighbour's driveway across the street, their cameras panning the crowd. A reporter was interviewing someone who was crying. Ham shut the curtains, paced for a few minutes, then opened the banking app on his phone to check the balances in his various accounts. That boosted his spirits.

By 3:45 p.m. all the major grocery stores had pulled Chinny-Chin-Chin products from their shelves. Whole Foods said they wouldn't even donate the products to a homeless shelter and planned to send everything to a landfill. Stock value plummeted. Sales of Newman's Own sauces, soups and stews jumped 17 per cent by the time the markets closed. Ham considered transferring some of his investment capital into Newman's Own, or into a private landfill company, but decided the optics wouldn't be good.

More people came forward saying that they, too, had found baby wolf teeth in their Chinny-Chin-Chin food. Some said they'd found what appeared to be tiny baby wolf claws. One man claimed to have found an actual wolf fetus in his Full Moon Marinara.

There was talk of a class-action lawsuit.

Karl was freaking out. Unlike Ham, who'd paid for his mansion in cash, Karl had mortgage payments. And he had a family. A kid who needed braces. A rotting front deck. A minivan that needed a new windshield.

"Breathe, Karl," said Ham. They'd been on the phone numerous times that afternoon. "Look. I've known hard times. I've had trouble on my roof before—a wolf at the door—and that turned out okay. You need to focus on getting us through this. Then we'll rebrand. Leverage the attention and spin it positive."

Ham didn't let on that he was nervous too. Not so much about the public shaming or its impact on the business. He knew that Joe Blow had nothing better to do but bat rich people's reputations around like shuttlecocks in cyberspace. And he knew that the markets went up and down. Money plus time equals redemption. His business sense would get him through. Also, he knew that scandals never lasted long. The public had a short attention span. Like the kind of attention span needed to build a house of straw. Or sticks.

What Ham was truly worried about was old-fashioned physical pain. When his brothers called him a wimp, they had a point. He was paranoid about injury. And now, there was an angry crowd stomping violently on his English lavender. It was a volatile mob. Unpredictable. Maybe they had weapons. What if they stormed his house? What if they hurt him? Ham was the kind of guy who shrieked for ten minutes straight when he stubbed his toe. Nearly threw up from the pain of a hangnail. In business, he was a bold entrepreneur. At home he was a strong, disciplined perfectionist. But when it came to matters of the flesh, he was as fragile as a bubble of soap.

Suddenly, there was a crash from the front hall.

"Hang on, Karl," he said and went to investigate, sneaking around the corner of the kitchen where the crowds wouldn't see him. A brick had been thrown through one of the windows into the solarium.

"What's happening?" said Karl. "Sir? Are you still there? Sir? It looks like CNN is on the story now."

There was a smell of smoke and sulphur; a stink bomb had been shoved through his mail slot. Footsteps sounded on his roof. The side door was shaking. Someone was trying to get in. Ham knew his mansion was no longer safe.

"Hello? Hello?" came Karl's voice through the phone. "Boss! Please! Talk to me!" Ham clenched his jaw. He didn't have the patience. No one was *at* Karl's house. No one was going to *attack* Karl. Karl was safe and sound in his little house, wherever it was, worrying only about himself and the future of his job.

"No more handholding, Karl. You're the director of communications. Go communicate," he said, and pressed *End Call*.

Like many of today's super smart and über-rich, Ham had commissioned a concrete safety bunker—a survival network—to be built under his mansion. It was somewhere to go in case of a nuclear war, a deadly contagion, a zombie apocalypse or an angry mob. Ham felt that anyone without a survival bunker under their house was simply irresponsible. If he didn't have one, what would he have done? Gone to Weiner and Hock's trailer for safety?

He opened the hidden latch behind the mirror on a false wall in the back of a guest bedroom closet, punched in the access code and climbed down a narrow secret staircase into the underground sanctuary. Through a periscopic camera that hung from the ceiling, he watched helplessly as someone stood on the edge of the decorative fountain in the middle of the driveway roundabout and peed into the water. Someone else was spray-painting *Bacon Time* on his garage door. Security officers and local law enforcement stood alongside the hooligans. They did nothing to stop the violence and vandalism. In fact, Ham thought he saw one uniformed HomeWise private guard hand a protester a rock. Or maybe it was an egg.

Disgusted, Ham turned off the camera, walked through the "Refuge and Relax" portion of the bunker and into the escape corridor, which led away from the property and eventually connected to the town's underground drainage system. The dark, musty corridor—essentially, a long tunnel—was illuminated by his emergency high-powered head lamp. It felt like it would never end. Ham kept checking behind him, but there was no one.

The corridor exited through an open sewer pipe in a culvert. He climbed up the ditch into an alleyway parking lot. It had been a long time since Ham had been anywhere besides his home, his head office on Burrard Street for meetings, and the inside of a taxicab between the two locales. This looked like the back of a strip mall. A bearded bald man in a Canucks jersey was leaning against Donut Delight's emergency exit door, flicking a lighter that wasn't working. A kid zoomed by on a skateboard—so close Ham could smell the marijuana embedded in his checkered flannel shirt. Someone's car alarm blared. There was a siren in the distance. A crow flew by with a Fudgsicle wrapper in its mouth.

Ham was still wearing the bathrobe he'd hastily donned when getting out of the hot tub and realized such a high-end piece of loungewear would inevitably draw attention. Before anyone looked his way, he scuttled up a pile of milk crates and old pallets to toss the six-hundred-dollar robe into a Dumpster. But when he peered over the edge of the bin, he became enveloped by the stench from a pile of half-eaten spring rolls, barbecued chicken, remnants of wonton soup and onion rings. Bits of a cream cheese bagel lay beside something orange in a squished Curry Up! takeout box. Flies buzzed around the food like bubbles around a glass of champagne.

Ham's snout started to quiver. It had been years since he'd last eaten rotting scraps. He closed his eyes and remembered his mother's gentle grunting as he and his brothers rooted with her through orange peels, eggshells and coffee filters back at their family pen. Before they'd been sent away to seek their fortunes without their dear mammy. Before they'd developed such contrasting work ethics and business smarts. Before they'd grown so far apart.

The memory came as a surprise. Ham had been so busy overseeing his gourmet food empire and blogging about his corporate philosophies he hadn't given a moment's thought to his brothers for over a year. He never talked about his earlier days or his family background. Yet in that moment he imagined the three siblings rolling playfully in the bin of grub, filthy and free. He felt a pang in his chest. It was his true self knocking on his hardened heart: *Let me in! Let me in!*

Ham climbed over the edge of the rusty blue bin, giddy with anticipation. But when he was halfway over, a piece of metal scraped along the flesh of his belly. He shrieked in agony. It happened so fast, and the pain was so intense—he imagined he must have been torn open from nipples to privates! Surely he would bleed to death. Twisting as he fell, he landed sideways in the soft pile of rotting food with a graceless *oomph.*

Ham lay there, writhing in pain. His bathrobe, which he could have used to wrap around the wound and stem the bleeding, lay just out of reach. Was this how his life would end? Is this how he would be found? Anonymous and dirty, like a poor homeless stray?

Eventually, he sucked his lower lip into his mouth and peered down along his midsection, expecting to see his own vital organs on full display through the gaping wound. They were not. He frowned and examined himself more closely. Finally, he saw the tiny white scrape. It looked as though it had been drawn on his skin with a piece of chalk. He rubbed the scratch, and it faded slightly.

He closed his eyes and let out a sigh.

Overwhelmed with relief and gratitude, Ham began to eat. He dug into the glorious pile of food with lust and joy, lifting his pale-pink face for breath only when he had to. He ate to reassure himself, to reward himself and to celebrate his courageous escape from peril. Noodles hung from one ear and a baby carrot poked out from a nostril. Like a turtle returning from the rocky beach to the salty seas, Ham felt he was finally home. He savoured each bite and chewed far more than was necessary. With each swallow, satisfaction travelled down his throat and into his soft, lima bean–shaped body. His eyes slowly drifted shut and his ears lay back against the sides of his head. Everything would be okay. He was a survivor. He rested his chin upon a squished Styrofoam takeout box half-full of ginger beef, nibbled a bit of something mustardy that was within reach of his lips, and, finally, Ham slept.

The moon shone like a tractor beam on his bristly hair, and the sound of his snores was amplified by the container walls.

With the dawn came a chorus of crows, barking dogs and delivery trucks beeping as they reversed. Ham groped around groggily for the remote control so he could turn on the news, but grabbed the mouldy end of a Seafood Sensation Subway sandwich instead. He pushed into it a few times, opened his eyes the rest of the way, then shook his head and remembered where he was: in a Dumpster.

Instead of crying over his situation, our hero looked at the mass of wasted, delicious food he was lying in and was overcome by a flash of inspiration he hoped both economists and chefs would later call visionary. He picked a piece of brown lettuce off one of his haunches and ate it.

This time, Ham would go back to his roots.

He'd package that which gave him comfort, joy and pleasure on a day of fear, distress and pain. It was so simple, it was perfect! He'd do with food waste what he'd done with a boiled predator just a few business cycles ago: market the shit out of it. Ham would just have to get Karl to draft a public apology for the baby wolf tooth incident, lay low until the current scandal faded away, then rebrand himself as the King of Upcycled Food. He'd even bring Weiner and Hock on board! His sibs knew the target market better than anyone, and the optics of the brothers teaming up would work like a charm. No doubt they could help source Dumpsters of compost and scraps all over the city. Maybe he'd even let them move into the mansion. They could live in the "Refuge and Relax" portion of the bunker. It could be a perk of their employment. The backstory was a brand specialist's wet dream. Rags to riches to scandal to born-again family man, all in the name of fraternity, forgiveness and overcoming the odds. Then, of course, back to riches once again!

In the time it took a crusty-eyed baker from Donut Delight to hurl a batch of day-olds into the bin, Ham had conceptualized a line of delicious, easy-to-prepare, compost-based meals for busy, low-income families and single under-employeds. In his head, he drafted a business plan. He tinkered with names, packaging and logo ideas.

It was environmental. It was economical. It was a nutrition choice that matched today's lifestyle. The food had been delicious once, why not ride the tide and profit from it a second time? He started crunching the numbers and giddily called his brothers' trailer in Pitt Meadows.

Reflection Time: Ten Questions for Discussion

1) What kind of siblings turn down a business opportunity of a lifetime that is both environmental, economical and nutritious?

   (a) lazy ones
   (b) simple-minded ones
   (c) ungrateful ones
   (d) all of the above

2) What steps have you personally taken to protect your brothers from their own bad decisions, lack of work ethic and short attention spans? (For example: sent them jars of gourmet food, offered them business opportunities almost too good to be true, etc.)

3) Have you ever eaten a Compost Cake™? If yes, did you enjoy it? If no, please list your other food sensitivities.

4) Do you blame Ham for pulling Compost Cake™'s advertising from *Delish* magazine after the article "Who Is Even Eating This Crap?" was published?

5) Do you think the disclaimer on Compost Cake™'s packaging went far enough in protecting people vulnerable to digestive issues?

6) Are you aware that food poisoning symptoms can be almost indistinguishable from the common flu?

7) Do you think collection agencies who prey on entrepreneurs who maybe just need a little more time to hone their business plan and tweak their product are scum of the earth?

8) Discuss "hard work," "imagination" and "overcoming odds."

9) Define "success" and provide specific examples.

10) Will you read Ham's tell-all memoir, *Happy at Last: Finding Joy in a Straw House*, when it is released by First Pig Press next fall?

Mary Wonderful's New Grimoire

In a cold cottage at the dark end of the woods lies a dying witch. By her side is a faithful cat. Thunder is normally a sleek feline with mustard-yellow eyes and fur as black as a moonless night. But the imminent death of his mistress has thrown the little puss for a loop. He has become depressed and has completely let himself go. His fur is mangy and matted and he has lost the will to even swat a cockroach.

Oh, don't think it's cute, a kitty cat "grieving" its dying owner. Cats are selfish beasts with about as much capacity for compassion as they have talent for typing. Thunder's state of mind is not based on love per se, but is directly related to how the hag's demise will affect her capacity to toss him scraps, to provide a soft lap for him to curl up in, or to scratch under his chin.

What about meeeeee? thinks the cat as the old witch exhales green smoke that smells like rancid poultry and burnt hair. Her complexion has become a much paler shade of mauve than usual and Thunder considers jabbing a pointy foreclaw into the skin of her neck to see if a little cream might seep through the puncture wound for him to enjoy.

"Do it!" a voice suddenly calls. The cat jumps two feet into the air and lands on the counter, face to face with the witch's daughter, Mary Wonderful. "Claw her! Why not? Stab her! Draw blood! Draw cream! Draw battery acid! No one cares about her now, and no one will care when she's dead!"

Mary Wonderful is a kindergarten teacher. Vegetarian. Has a schnauzer named Happy. Sings in a choir. Lives in a condo decorated in a simple, Japanese motif. She named herself; forged the paperwork on her birth certificate because her mother hadn't bothered to name the child whom she didn't really expect to live. Mary hasn't been back to the cottage since the day she escaped through the chimney when she was a toddler. But she suspected the old boot was on her last legs because of a telltale rainbow that had appeared in the sky over the shack recently.

You? thinks the cat. *What are* you *doing here?*

Mary Wonderful plucks Thunder off the counter and chucks him to the floor. Sometimes she wishes she did not have the ability to read the minds of animals.

"I'm here to collect what is rightfully mine."

The cat hisses, then skulks off to hide under the stove.

A typical daughter, upon seeing her mother at death's door, face twisted in agony, body riddled with disease and infection, would sit with the woman, offer a few words of comfort, hold her shrivelled hand or brush her thin hair.

But not Mary Wonderful. That's not why she's come. You see, all witches keep a diary—a daily record of spells, rituals, recipes, incantations and other magical information. It is called a grimoire, and collecting it is the only reason Mary Wonderful is here.

Why does she want such a book? Surely not to cast spells of her own. Mary Wonderful, who dresses in pastels and gets headaches from candlelight, has turned her back on all things witch.

Will she tuck the grimoire away in her storage locker? A memento of her heritage and genealogy? Will she donate it to the Canadian Museum of Sorcery where historians and gawkers can learn about dark power in a sterile and supervised environment? Perhaps she'll sell the book to a wealthy private investor and buy herself a time-share in Mexico.

Mary Wonderful has considered all these options, but she has made up her mind to take the book out of circulation—to destroy the grimoire—so no one can read her mother's words and know her secrets. It's the only way Mary Wonderful's true identity as the daughter of a witch can be finally and permanently erased. Whether to hurl it into the ocean, bury it under a tree or drop it into a stoneware kiln to be incinerated has yet to be decided. First, she needs to find the thing.

The place is a disaster. Witches are terrible housekeepers, and this one is also a hoarder. There are bags of bones and boxes of buttons. Food scraps and beeswax. Birchbark and bike parts. Crumpled silk and rotting milk. Under floorboards are mushrooms; in the drawer, a dead duck. As for the grimoire? Alas, no luck.

After hours of searching, Mary Wonderful stands in the middle of the mess, hands on her hips, and listens to the crone's raspy breath. She wonders if the book even exists. Perhaps it's a myth that all witches document their lives. Perhaps her mother's just lazy.

She is about to give up when the cat reappears, dragging a leather-bound volume across the floor by strings used to tie the cover shut.

You looking for this? thinks Thunder. Oh sure, he could have brought the grimoire out sooner, but you know how cats are.

Mary Wonderful snatches the book. She plans to dash straight home, but flips it open for a quick peek first. She is shocked by what she reads.

> *April 2*
>
> *Dear child, love of my heart, charm of my soul. I see that you have found a foster family. I am so happy that…*

What? She flips to another page.

> *June 13*
>
> *Good luck on your final exams! I'm placing my Brilliance Spell on you so you'll get all* As*!*

How could this be?

> *November 18*
>
> *Oh, daughter, you changed your hair! I loved it long, but the short, spiky look suits you as well!*

It's not a grimoire, but an extended love letter. A scrapbook. A dedication from a witch to the daughter who considered herself a motherless child. The old woman must have disguised herself and watched her every move, thinks Mary Wonderful. Of course! She is a sorceress, able to transfigure at will. She turns to the last page.

> *My only wish is to see my beloved girl, my only child, my angel, before I die. To feel her close to me and tell her I love her. To give her*

The handwriting trails off.

Mary looks at her mother on the rusty, rickety bed in the cold cottage and begins to wail. "Oh, Mother! I'll never forgive myself for forsaking you!"

And then, ever so slowly, the witch's eyelids rise.

Mary gasps. "You're awake!" She puts a hand upon her heart.

The muscles in the old woman's neck strain like a net full of fish as she struggles to lift her head. Her lips quiver. She is trying to speak.

"What? What is it, Mother?" Mary Wonderful leans close. The smell is nauseating, but she doesn't turn away. The witch's crooked pointer finger curls up, motioning for her daughter to come closer still.

Then her eyelids wilt shut again.

"No! Please! Don't die!" Mary Wonderful wraps her arms around the old woman and lifts her to her chest. She is thin and brittle. It feels as if she might snap like a twig. Mother and daughter are forehead to forehead, nose to nose. "You loved me!" Mary Wonderful sobs. "All this time, you truly loved me!"

Their faces are so close that when the old witch opens her mouth, the girl doesn't see the spider crawl up her mother's tongue, over her rotten bottom teeth and onto her cracked lip. It is a beautiful spider. Black, with silver hairs. Like a piece of jewellery. An heirloom.

She feels her mother's muscles slacken and her body go limp. She doesn't feel the spider pull itself along on a thread of spun silk it has lashed from the old woman's dry, grey mouth into her own wet, pink one. She feels a tickle in her throat as the spider enters, but because she's sobbing and carrying on about not being a good daughter, about how she wants more time with her mother now and blah, blah, blah, she doesn't feel the little arachnid go down, down, down.

Mary Wonderful lays the witch's dead body back onto the rusty, rickety bed and takes a seat in the rocking chair by the stove. She scratches Thunder under his chin and he settles into her warm, soft lap. He purrs as she opens the leather grimoire, whose bewitched pages no longer read like a love letter from mother to daughter, but have been transformed back into a record of spells, rituals, recipes, incantations and other magical information. The cat licks the fur on his foreleg as his new mistress flips to the section with instructions on what to do with the corpse of a witch whose soul has been reincarnated into the body of a young kindergarten teacher.

East O

Conditions were crowded in East Ovary.

Imagine a quarter million eggs, each tethered to the rubbery pod wall by her own personal follicle, all squeezed together into a space the size of the twist-off cap from a two-litre bottle of Canada Dry. Honestly, you couldn't swing a papillomavirus around in there without hitting someone in the corona radiata. But we didn't complain. We were evenly spaced and everyone got along fairly well. We avoided calling it "cramped," with its negative cultural stigma, and instead referred to our East O home as "cozy."

Looking back, we all agreed those first twelve years were the best. Just a gaggle of mini-goddesses we were, hanging out with friends, gossiping, singing, copying your games and inventing our own, discussing our destinies and listening to Blood's tales. We didn't have a care in the world.

And neither did you, back then!

Blood said that West Ovary was pretty much a clone of us—same numbers, same layout, same "level of immaturity" (her words). We didn't appreciate the character generalization. We also didn't like being called a "clone." With a population like ours, individuality was troublesome enough, especially for the ones whose DNA was being recycled for the umpteenth time.

"Okay, okay. West O isn't *really* a replica of you guys. Their pod faces the other way and they're farther from her heart," said Blood. "But I stand by 'lazy.'"

We were all a bit jealous of Blood, who spent day and night travelling through you, visiting your heart, brain, muscles. She knew everything that was going on in your body and life, and she spread the news wherever she went. You had no secrets from Blood, and she'd spill her guts every chance she could. She was our eyes and ears into your eyes and ears.

Not everyone was cut out for life here in East O. The darkness, the humidity, the lack of privacy, the vague smell of sulphur and rust in the pod, and the realization that the chances of personally meeting a strong, long-tailed foreigner and initiating the Nine-Month Project were virtually squat—it was all too much for some to bear. About a thousand of us called it quits every day. Pulled the plug. Kicked the ladybucket. The rest couldn't agree whether to call it suicide, bad luck or simply a lack of ambition. According to Blood, the same thing was going on in West O. Immature siblings would release their cytoplasm, suffocate their own nucleus, shrivel up and dissolve away.

At the risk of sounding harsh, we didn't have much sympathy for the giver-uppers. They were short-term thinkers. Party poopers. Pathetic, really. "Let 'em go," we'd say. "It's their decision. More room for the rest of us."

Those of us who were in it for the long haul were frisky, ticklish, pink and carefree. Optimistic and easygoing. Not unlike *you* back then, when your days were filled with playing "office" and making up reasons for your Barbies to sue each other. When you were in elementary school, you loved those classic games: wink murder, twenty questions and the favourite—truth or dare.

We had our own version of that last one, with slightly modified rules. Instead of memory-based truths (which we were lacking, having not actually lived lives yet), we had to say something about the future. A few of us called the game "speculation or dare," until an egg with DNA from Madame

Blavatsky told us to stop disrespecting our siblings' visions. We all had specific wisdom based on our spirit lives, she said. Call them accurate hunches. Glimmers of our destinies. They were more than speculation: these glimmers counted as truth. It didn't matter if the thing had yet to occur. It would, and that was enough. It made sense, what she said. There were things we kind of just knew.

"Truth or dare?" we called out one day as you were riding your bike to Shy-Anne's house.

It was Florence's turn. Another one with strong, pre-named genes.

"Truth!" We weren't surprised at her selection. No one had chosen dare yet, either here at home or (apparently) over in West O.

"I will save our lady's marriage," Ms. Nightingale announced. "At least for a while."

We were intrigued. It was fun thinking about the power we had. We'd piece together these declarations to try to figure out what your life would look like, and what part we'd play.

The next time: "Truth or dare?"

"My turn!" said an ovum named Lucille Ball. "Here's a truth: She'll be excused from the grade eight fitness test in gym because of me."

We all laughed when Lucy put on a fake little high-pitched voice and wobbled around in her follicle. "I can't do it, Mr. Eccles! I have to go lie down! It's a girl thing! You don't understand," she cried, imitating you playing up your PMS symptoms for your phys. ed. teacher.

A few weeks later, when you and Shy-Anne were practising cartwheels in her backyard, it was time again: "Truth or dare?"

"I choose to reveal a truth," said Teresa.

"Gosh-golly! Are you *sure?*"

"Yes. I am sure." Teresa was known for her compassion and empathy, not her ability to pick up on sarcasm. "Now is not the time for dares. Our woman is a mere eight years old. She is not ready."

She swung in her follicle, looked into the middle distance and spoke in a thick Indian accent. "Here is a thing I know to be true: up to seventeen of us will be artificially matured and removed from our home with the use of chemical warfare and violence. It will be called a 'harvest,' but it will occur in the springtime. We will be flash-frozen and stored in darkness for many, many years."

Everyone shut up.

The only sounds that could be heard were a distant *thump* from your North-Northeastern Quadrant and the occasional *pop* of a membrane somewhere far away. Even Blood was quiet as she whooshed past, eavesdropping.

"Our woman will consider us her insurance plan," said Teresa. "But when she finally tries to engage us, we will die upon thawing. Our lifeless shells will be put into a yellow plastic bin marked *Biomedical Waste* and promptly incinerated. It will be a pity." She tilted downward, as if in prayer. "It will be a shame."

We had no reason not to believe her. She carried the sainthood DNA. She'd never been able to even bring herself to exaggerate, let alone tell a whopper like that if it wasn't true. She was so straightforward and honest that she won every staring contest we'd ever held.

Obviously we were horrified. Everyone started sobbing. Blood, the perpetual busybody, told West O exactly what Teresa had said, and they started sobbing too. Well, with all that bawling and carrying on from your ovaries, it's no wonder you doubled over in pain. Your mother thought you might have ruptured an appendix and took you to a walk-in clinic, but in the end they chalked it up to gas.

Our tears didn't last long. We soon realized that even if what the nun egg said were true, it wouldn't be the end of the world. Because as bad as biomedical waste and incineration sounded, there *were* a lot of us. We could play games and tell jokes and share truths and speculations until the cows came home, but the hard reality was this: of the fraction of us who would mature, only a pinch would—*might!*—became zygotes. We knew that pretty much everyone, whether from East O or West, whether a pessimist with a death wish or a dreamer with big plans, would end up wasted.

Flushed.

Absorbed.

Wrapped in toilet paper and stuffed into a brown paper bag lining a metal waste receptacle.

Statistically, more of us would become stains on bedsheets or panties than would become human offspring. That was our reality.

After Teresa's downer bombshell, we organized a pep rally to raise morale. We chanted slogans about life being precious and short, and living in the moment and taking things day by day and us being the seeds of humanity, and the need for us to stay healthy and strong, for the greater good. They must have heard the racket over in West O, but instead of sending Blood over to tell us to take it down a notch, they started chanting right along with us—their muffled voices floated through the membranes and tissues of your body like alcohol through the liver. You told Shy-Anne you felt like you had butterflies in your stomach. You told her you felt you were being tickled from the inside. It made you want to do a round-off back handspring right then and there.

In the spring of your thirteenth year we started getting reports of some weird occurrences throughout your body. According to Blood, everything was going haywire. We thought our messenger was just jittery and paranoid, maybe from all the grande chocolate frappuccinos you'd been sharing with Shy-Anne and some other kids in your grade seven class every day after school.

"Don't blame Starbucks," said Blood. "This is some serious shit."

We'd never heard her swear before, so we listened up. Apparently Pituitary Gland was acting like God's gift to you, making up random new rules and trying to boss everyone around. In retaliation, Acne had annexed your face and your breasts had become tender, lumpy dough balls, one noticeably larger than the other.

"On top of all that, Sweat Glands are stuck on turbo," Blood told us. "Tear Ducts are leaking for no reason at all, and there's hair popping out of perfectly innocent pores. It's friggin' anarchy around here."

Despite Blood's reports, we tried to carry on as before. But the next time we played our game, Joan of Arc, small and brave, cleared her throat, puffed up her chest and boldly said, "Dare."

We knew we were due for someone to bypass truth and try a dare, but still it came as a surprise to us when, without even an "*Au revoir, mes amies*," Joanie burst out of her follicle, launched herself into the abyss and tumbled toward the seaweedy fringes of the dark tunnel.

We held our breath and clung to the edges of our follicles. No one actually thought she'd meet a spunky foreigner who would change the course of everything. But still. Now that a dare was in motion, anything was possible.

Twenty-seven hours later, Joan, our friend and hero, died and dribbled in a stream of watery brown-pink blood through your lime-green bikini bottoms and down your inner thighs when you emerged from Clearwater Lake after a game of Marco Polo with five or six kids from school. Someone's kind, observant aunt ran to you with a *Smurf's Up!* beach towel, wrapped it around your waist and shuffled you to the change room, but not before Gordie Doucette said, "Jenny's on the ra-ag! Jenny's on the ra-ag!" so loudly that everyone on the beach turned your way.

Blood saw the whole thing through your eyes. She denied responsibility and claimed it wasn't her department, said she shouldn't be blamed for that particular catastrophe. "I go where I'm needed, do what I'm told," she told us. "It wasn't my fault your little ovum didn't have a more appropriate sense of what is personal and what is public."

We really were sorry to have caused you such embarrassment, but we had no choice. There's no convenient first time. We did try to warn you one of us was on the way, but how were you to know the meaning of cramps and bloating and a dull lower-back ache?

We pledged to time our games and the dares to coincide with the moon's rhythms. West O agreed that this was a good idea. That way, you'd be able to predict and prepare for the sad wreckage of a daring egg that chose to take the leap each month. Unless, of course, fertilization were to occur—a highly unlikely prospect at your age and considering our culture's negative attitude toward sexual intercourse with girls on the fresh side of fertility. But don't get me started on society's wasteful and ignorant bias against teenage pregnancy, two words that are more often preceded by "unwanted" than "blessed."

Despite what Pituitary Gland was trying to encourage us to do, for the next few lunar cycles, we went back to only sharing truths. ("I will delay my journey into Fallopia for an extra forty-eight hours, avoiding conception after a sambuca-fuelled night with a bike courier," and "I ruin her flax-linen capri pants," and "She'll be so happy to see me, she'll whisper 'Thank Christ!' from a stall in the Supreme Court washroom, third floor.")

Eventually, we knew it was time for another dare. Martha piped up. "Later, gators!" said little Ms. Graham before she arched her torso, shut her eyes, dramatically curled into herself like a dandelion at night and leaped.

By this time, you knew what to expect. You'd read the

book *Our Bodies, Ourselves* that your mother gave you. Shy-Anne, already a *C* cup, was four months older. She was wise and talkative. She insisted her boyfriend wear two condoms, with built-in spermicide.

And so it went. Sometimes the daring egg matured and leaped from East O, sometimes from West. By the following Christmas, we became so regular you'd think the moon revolved its cycles around *us*.

In high school, you weren't much interested in boys. Oh, they were interested in you, but you always seemed to have urgent homework, or a babysitting job, or something going on with Community Youth Council.

"They're all losers at our school," you told Shy-Anne. She called you a snob. You called her a slut, and you didn't speak for almost two months.

With your attitude, we knew that our chances of meeting a mini-tadpole along the monthly journey were precisely zilch. It made for a lonely trip south for those who dared. A silent descent in a quiet elevator. A starless night.

But never mind. It was your choice, and we respected that you weren't looking to have us fertilized back then. We knew you had other plans, and we told ourselves our expiration dates were a long way away.

When you were twenty-one, our dear Mary planted herself on your ovary and swelled up like a pimple. You moaned like you were dying, but were determined to write your LSAT despite the pain. Your doctor said it was a follicular cyst, assured you that it wasn't uncommon and told you to take some Advil and get plenty of rest. The doctor said surgery would be a last resort; that these things usually cleared up on their own after a few days. Mary had a lot of baggage in her DNA regarding the whole virginity thing. She swore there were better ways for us to serve you than wait to allow ourselves to be "invaded by wriggling heathens" in the tube. We tried to reason with her, to talk her down, but she started going on about miracles and angels and heavenly fathers. She told us not to be afraid. We all thought she was off her rocker. Anyhow, your doctor was right. Mary's protest didn't last long. When she dried up, a few of us were sad, but mostly everyone, including Blood, was relieved that surgery would not be required.

Doing the math backwards, we figured that Shy-Anne's first zygote must have taken hold on the New Year's Eve after she turned twenty-three. By that summer she was enormous. You lay in the sun with her on the shore of Clearwater Lake one afternoon between classes and couldn't keep your eyes off her ripe belly, her purple-silver stretch marks and the line of downy hair that pointed down from her navel. She asked you if you wanted to feel the baby kicking. You wrinkled your nose and put your hand there because you didn't want to be rude.

A baby boy was born. We all sang and swayed at the baby shower, but you didn't feel us. Or you did, and just ignored us. You didn't reach out to hold him when he was passed around or let him squeeze your finger or fall asleep in your lap. "Someone else can burp him, thanks," you said. "I'd probably drop the kid." You gave him a sterling silver rattle, engraved with his initials.

Shy-Anne withdrew from law school. You went on the pill.

"Why? Oh why?" we cried, knowing full well why, but wishing you'd change your mind. Our awareness of the situation was short-lived. Soon the whole lot of us were duped into thinking you were pregnant. Talk about a false sense of accomplishment. We were all like: "OMG! Now she's gonna start shopping for baby things! She's gonna start redecorating! She's gonna research kindergartens!" It was as if we were all there hiding behind the couch at a surprise party waiting for the guest of honour to arrive, party hats on, noisemakers at the ready, half-drunk, shushing each other with fingers upon lips. But no one showed up. It was no one's birthday. There was no party.

In hindsight: *duh*. We should have believed Blood. There was nothing to celebrate at all.

During that dark era, no one matured and no one left East or West O. Life was pretty surreal—everyone was wound up tight, waiting anxiously for this non-existent zygote to develop.

When you finally let your prescription lapse and gave us the green light to follow the moon's cycles again, you were with a man who had no stars in his Milky Way.

"A *vasectomy?*" said Shy-Anne. "He's thirty-three years old! Same as you! Don't you *ever* want to be a mother?" She was pregnant with twins. "Motherhood is the best. You seriously don't know what you're missing."

"Oh yes I do," you said and hung up the phone. That weekend you went to Martinique with the neutered fellow. He had a time-share there.

Well, *we* heard Shy-Anne, and several years later, the night you dallied with the Crown prosecutor nineteen years your senior, we sent our big gun on the dare: Marilyn. And lo and behold, it worked! The squinty-eyed lawyer's man-spore penetrated Ms. Monroe's cell membrane. She knew what to do instinctually and nestled herself into the soft, cushy lining Blood had so lovingly prepared. A satisfied hush fell over us. A common purpose was achieved. We were a happy colony.

But you received the zygote with a cold, cold heart.

Blood told us you were relieved to have the freedom to choose, but oh, how we wept when M was eradicated.

Did you regret it? Did you ever yearn for someone who'd be like you? Someone to worry about? Who'd have your beautiful hazel eyes and curly hair? Your long second toe? Your work ethic and high IQ? Did you wonder about who would sit with you when you became old and useless? Did you ever think of names?

We figured eventually you would.

Sure enough, the April after you turned thirty-five you were researching fertility clinics. "We *told* you so!" came the chorus, but we were scolded for being smug. It wasn't that you regretted dealing with Marilyn so hastily, said Blood. It was just a matter of leaving your options open so you could focus on your other goals without ruling out having a family. It was a matter of careful planning. For future considerations.

But Teresa shuddered and we remembered what she had foretold. We all knew how things would end up. We did what we could to get the message to you, but when was the last time you listened to your gut, let alone your ovaries?

You could have paid the $21,500 fee to New Hope Reproductive Technology Centre in cash, but you decided to put it on Visa instead. May as well get the Air Miles points. The brochure in the lobby said *Conceive of This!*

You gritted your teeth and made "prick" jokes as the doctor gave you the injections.

He called it a "follicle-stimulating hormone."

We called it a "rave."

Ooh la la! Whatever it was, we were like, *Bring it on!* We felt invincible. Daring. Mature and ready to take on the world. We were so hopped up on the drug, we danced day and night, night and day. It was friggin' Ibiza!

The party ended abruptly with the appearance of a hissing transvaginal aspirator.

"Harvest time," said Teresa, who had known it all along. "God be with you." And with a sickening pop and a slurp she was sucked into the vacuum syringe. A handful of others followed closely behind.

The doctor then injected you with more drugs, this time to sober us up. Jolt us back to reality. Talk about the hangover from hell.

We knew we'd never see Teresa and the others again. Marie Curie tried to comfort us. "Vitrification's nothing," she said. "They're frozen stiff. They can't feel a damn thing."

No one mentioned the yellow plastic bin.

You became one of the top family law attorneys in the city. You spent your days negotiating terms of agreement about whether five-year-old kids with their own iPads and nannies and designer backpacks would spend Christmas with Mom in Maui or with Dad in Whistler. It paid well, and you bought a house by the university with a garden and an ocean view. You wore tailored suits and went to fine restaurants. Handsome lovers abounded but you weren't willing to risk giving any of us a chance. You installed a copper antenna that was like kryptonite to sperm, killing or maiming them in their squiggly tracks. That was uncomfortable for you, so you had it removed. Blood told us you tried an arm implant next, until you couldn't handle the weight gain.

However, none of the handsome lovers stayed long. It seemed they all wanted to change you in some way. Make you more domestic, less dominating. They wanted to take you to their favourite places. They weren't as interested in yours. Even the hot young landscaper with the spiky blond hair and the tanned abs who followed you around and gave you flowers he'd personally grown ended up being kind of a jerk. *Good riddance*, we thought, for he was also a cyclist, and none of his single-celled rovers had the juice to properly present themselves in our little domain of fortune.

But when it came right down to it, life was busy and dating was tedious. You wondered how other people had time for relationships. Between work, overseeing kitchen renos, Pilates and book club, you didn't even get past creating a username for Plenty of Fish. You decided it wasn't worth the trouble and became virtually celibate when you were made partner at the law firm. All those clever tricks and devices meant to thwart the foreigners or trick us into altered states were rendered pointless.

Co-workers didn't understand. They took pity on you. Some thought you were gay and suggested mountain biking clubs you could join. Others thought you were too picky and offered up their brothers, sons, widowed fathers and exes.

None of this mattered much to us though. By now, we had almost reached "meh" ourselves. We knew that destiny sometimes skips a generation, and we figured we'd have to wait until the next go-round for our incarnations.

Your mother phoned to tell you Shy-Anne's twins were graduating from high school. You were happy for her, sent an e-card and went on another corporate leadership retreat.

Then, at forty-six: *sis-boom-bah!* You fell in love.

He was a lean, wavy-haired mandolin player who lived in a tiny house far from everything. He grew pot in a red planter box on the windowsill. He made his own muesli, wrote haiku and ate kelp straight off the beach. You undressed with the light on, because he loved to watch.

He called you an angel, and you called New Hope Reproductive Technology Centre to set up an appointment. But as Teresa had predicted, there was a problem in the thawing process. We already knew what was to become of those pricey ice cubes that held our sisters.

You needed us, your remaining eggs. We were your last hope.

"Come on, eggs!" you cried. "Work with me here."

Ah, but we were so dang tired. Thoroughly pooped. And we'd lost track of the moon's rhythms altogether.

"No, no, no!" you cried. "It's not too late. We can do this!" You wanted to make him happy. This mandolinist. This poet. This wavy-haired new husband. You cursed our betrayal, then begged for our co-operation. You made demands. You even prayed. "Where is your sense of adventure?" you asked. "Your sense of loyalty? Of duty?" You did everything to try and persuade us: Spirulina. Maca. Royal jelly. Hot yoga. After sex you'd prop your legs up the wall to make it easier for the swimmers—never mind how dizzy it made your own Blood.

We applauded your efforts, and honestly, we tried. We held another pep rally and after a bit of *rah, rah, rah*, everyone agreed to give it their best go. They had a rally over in West O too. Someone must have made a speech; we thought we heard some clapping and whistling. Freshly motivated, some of us partnered up, matured as best they could and took the leap in pairs. In threes, even. But fertility's a bitch! It's complicated! It's exhausting! We didn't have the energy or the attention spans we used to. Like you and Pilates. Sometimes, we forgot what we were supposed to be doing and just lay down for a nap. We, too, cried for no reason now and then. We, too, wondered why someone had cranked up the heat.

And then Florence came forward.

We remembered what she'd told us all those years ago about almost saving your marriage.

She jumped, and we sang and swayed, elated. She met the hippie's sperm, welcomed it into her warm cytoplasm and became a diploid. It was a frigging miracle! One last kick at the conception can. But after two and a half cross-fingered months, she couldn't hold on any longer and ended up drowning in the toilet bowl.

Soon after, you left the plinky stoner musician and his squeaky Murphy bed and called Shy-Anne, who was still wise, freshly divorced and even more talkative. She was an empty-nester now and you found company in her conversation and pleasure in her company. Over a pitcher of sangria, you told her you wished you'd been sluttier when you were younger. She told you she wished she'd been pickier.

Eager for sisterhood and adventure, you took a sabbatical from your prestigious job, cashed in decades' worth of travel points and set out to see the world with your old friend. You floated naked in the Dead Sea. Yodelled, drunk, in the Swiss Alps. Hot-air ballooned at sunrise over Luxor, long grey hair blowing like the tassels on a child's bike handle, flirting with the dark-eyed pilot the whole way.

Yet despite this zest for life and the many interesting people you've encountered, your libido barely makes the radar these days. We haven't had a visitor up the tube since who knows when. A pep rally now just seems like a lot of work. And what would be the point? Blood still rushes by as consistent as ever. She takes her role of conduit seriously, gossiping endlessly about your adventures and misadventures, about the things you see and hear and say. It doesn't matter to her whether we are paying attention or not. Maybe Blood was right. Maybe we are just lazy. No one plays the old games anymore, here or in West O. So many of us just gave up.

They never did mature; never made the trip. Just shrivelled up on their follicles and were reabsorbed. Wasted.

But not me.

I'm the last viable egg in your dehydrated old body.

I'm still in the game, despite the fact that there's no one around who gives two shakes about truth and destiny, let alone daring acts of faith anymore. No one to impress. No one to cheer me on, or even give me a little shove. Pituitary Gland and Hypothalamus have written the whole lot of us off. Although I wouldn't call it a wasteland here, it's certainly no circus. But it's what we called home, and it holds a lot of memories and visions. It was the launch pad for our daring existence.

Now, it's only me. It's my turn. I guess I'd always known I'd be the last egg. And *la-dee-dah*, I am ready to go.

So I put on my best purple, with a red hat that doesn't go, and tango off the tip of my follicle. I sing as I float, loud and off pitch. I choose my own path, bypass the tube of Fallopia and waft through your universe like an astronaut without a rocket. A dandelion seed head in dry wind.

The Pull of Old Rat Creek

Fortune from Peking Moon Express fortune cookie
Be wary of that which clings to you.

---

www.geomagneticphenomenon.ca
According to the Canadian Space Weather Forecast Centre (CSWFC), solar flares associated with geomagnetic storms in the current eleven-year sun cycle (not as strong as the unprecedented 1959 space-weather events, but certainly more intense, at least initially, than the flare of 2003) produced an electromagnetic coronal mass ejection (CME) from the sun's surface on 03/04/2016. NASA monitored the cloud of charged solar particles as it travelled the approximately 150 million kilometres from sun to Earth. Although cosmic dispersion minimized global impact when the CME burst into Earth's magnetic field on 03/07/2016 at 18:22 Pacific Standard Time, powerful, concentrated electromagnetic fluctuations in the troposphere were directed over a single point in a sparsely populated location in south-central British Columbia. Satellite images indicate the nearest population centre to be Old Rat Creek (pop. 2,558). Town officials did not record any disturbances in power grids, radio communication or GPS.

CN Rail
Confidential Health and Safety Incident File, M. Perkins
Released in accordance with the Canadian Freedom of Information Act
08/13/2016

Margery Perkins, forty, assistant manager of paint at the Old Rat Creek Hardware Store in Old Rat Creek, BC, was walking along the (decommissioned) 754-B railway line between 18:00 and 18:30 on Friday, March 7, 2016. She was eating a takeout spring roll from Peking Moon Express. The item was wrapped in aluminum foil. Her purse contained six Hershey's Kisses, nine bobby pins, a pair of nail clippers, a tube of Dermalove psoriasis cream and a copy of *Ten Things a Recovering Alcoholic Needs to Know in Order to Stay Sober.* She wore small hoop earrings (sterling silver), and a gold chain with a tiny locket (gold-plated) that read *Mom.* The oldest of her five silver (amalgam) fillings (upper left, second bicuspid, circa 1989) was partially cracked and needed replacement.

On a separate track, approximately 2.3 kilometres from where Ms. Perkins was walking, two freight trains, one loaded with iron ore (southbound), the other with magnetic (coking) coal (northbound), passed each other. (Because it was a single-track line, one train—in this case, the one containing the iron ore—waited in the siding.) Their overlap occurred between 18:21 and 18:23.

Ms. Perkins later told medical personnel she had looked at her phone at 18:22, at the same time as she bit down on what she thought was a piece of spring roll but in fact was an approximately two-centimetre section of aluminum foil. The foil became temporarily lodged in the crack of her broken filling. A nerve was engaged, and a bolt of pain shot up the side of her head. The pain distracted her and caused her to lose her balance. She fell backwards, dropped the spring roll onto a railway tie, hit her head on the metal rail and apparently lost consciousness. Vibrations from the passing iron ore car and the magnetic coal car would have travelled along the track. The aluminum foil-amalgam filling nerve corruption combined with the concentrated electromagnetic fluctuations instigated by recorded solar activity and the energy of the passing railcars (transmitted through the line into Ms. Perkins's body) appear to have caused substantial changes to her ionic composition at the molecular level.

It is impossible to measure the physiological impact (if any) of electrical impulses from her cellphone, which rang (ringtone: "Radar") fifteen times before she regained consciousness. The caller, Naomi McFadden (forty-six, soap maker), did not leave a voice message, but sent two text messages. The first read simply *TGIF* and was followed by an emoji of a dancing woman in a long red dress. The second read, *Disco for Jesus. It's Singles Mingle Night at my church. You in?*

Tybalt Shapiro (thirty-three, percussionist for local band Satan's Ballsack), was riding his bike along the railway tracks and discovered Ms. Perkins lying with the left side of her head on the railroad track at 18:40. She was conscious but disoriented. ("She was off her tree. Staring into space like she was stoned. There was some drool," he reported.) Once Ms. Perkins was able to walk without dizziness, Mr. Shapiro accompanied her to the Old Rat Creek Walk-In Medical Clinic where she was treated for a mild concussion and sent home.

—Compiled with files from Old Rat Creek Walk-In Medical Clinic Patient Admission Report, CN Rail incident report, Smile Bright! Dentistry, iPhone records (from Apple Inc.) and Tybalt Shapiro's "A Drummer's Day" blog.

Old Rat Creek Walk-In Medical Clinic, March 7, 2016
Patient: Margery Perkins
Address: Unit 9, 2975 Pine Grove Lane, Old Rat Creek, BC, V0N 2K8
BC CareCard Personal Health No: 3498 480 292
Presenting symptoms of: *mild concussion*
Pupils: *slightly dilated*
Level of consciousness: *coherent*
Headache: *present, not acute*
BP: *130/80—within range*
Heart rate: *71 bpm—within range*
Patient released at 20:22
Note of Interest: *Metal instruments (stethoscope, medical penlight, arm of reflex hammer) appear to be slightly drawn to patient's skin, causing great interest among staff. No voiced complaints.*

Magic Mini Whiteboard Message
Mom, I made a pizza. You missed my soccer game. Sleeping over at Felix's.
Love, Owen
PS we lost 3–1.

Email Message
From: Margery
To: Doug
March 8, 8:15 a.m.

Hi Doug,
Sorry but I slipped walking home yesterday and whacked my noggin on the train track.

What a klutz! Had to go to the clinic. OK if I take today off?
—M

Sent from my iPhone

The Weekly Ratter

LOCAL REAL ESTATE MARKET PLUMMETS

Maya Ruth, Staff Writer

Since the closing of BritCo United Pulp and Paper Mill in January, a move that put 102 Rat Creek and area residents out of work, the number of houses (including single-family houses, townhouses and condominiums) on the market in the town of Old Rat Creek and in the Old Rat Creek Regional District has quadrupled. Some desperate homeowners are asking 25–30 per cent lower than assessed market value.

"It's a good time to buy," said realtor Helene DuBois. "People are dropping their prices. They're desperate. They're willing to take a loss just to finalize a sale."

Frankie Darkhorse, a former millwright, said, "That mill closing was a grave blow to the whole town. I don't know if we're ever going to get our mojo back."

*****TELUS** **8:23 AM** **72%**

Naomi

You missed a good Singles Mingle
last night. Pastor Kirk was asking about you.

Doubt that.

It's true!

Where were you?

Not feeling good.
Still in bed.

Don't tell me...

NO. Not hungover.

Cuz if so, I would have to kill you.

I know.

Wanna go for coffee? donuts? chat?

Not today. Maybe next week.

Remember: there's no chemical
solution to a spiritual problem.

Email Message
From: Doug
To: Margery
March 8, 8:31 a.m.

Hope you're feeling better quickly. I figure it'll be slow again today so take 'er easy. I'll get Norm to cover Paint for you.
See you tomorrow.
—D

PS I trust we're not getting back into old habits...

Sent from my iPhone

Magic Mini Whiteboard Message

Dear Owen,

Sorry about missing your game. Doug had me and Norm stay late to do inventory. I'm taking the day off to catch up on my sleep. Exhausted! Later gator.

Love, Mom

---

www.askarealscientist.com

Can People Really Become Magnetic?

Posted in The British Society of Skeptics (Spring 2016 Newsletter)

Tags: magnetic people, charisma, pseudo-science, skepticism, sticky people

People sometimes wonder: Is there such a thing as a magnetic person? Of course, we're not talking about someone with a magnetic personality, someone who is charismatic and attracts attention wherever they go. It's true that individuals can have magnetic personalities, even if they don't really do anything to deserve the attention or attraction.

No. We're talking here about people who claim their body generates a strong magnetic field. Supporters of pseudo-science and the occult would say, "Yes! Of course people can become magnetic. Long live Magneto!"

But well-informed skeptics and bona fide scientists know that these claims are rubbish. There is no scientific evidence to support the possibility of a person becoming magnetic. Consult a Gaussmeter. It will register zero and you'll know: it's just a trick.

Click on this video link to see for yourself what these charlatans are claiming: www.humanmagnets.com

It's obvious that all these supposedly "magnetic" people are leaning backwards slightly. Even the elderly Asian man with the iron on his chest is merely balancing it there. And who among us hasn't breathed on a spoon and had it stick to his or her nose? It's the warm vapour! That woman in the video with the coins and razor blades stuck flat to her back? Take a close look. See that sheen? She's clammy all over! Dust her with baby powder and see if that ten pence still sticks to the underside of her arm. It's a scientific fact that some people just have plain old sticky skin.

Try this: approach a supposedly magnetic person with a compass. If they are truly magnetic, the compass will go spinning wildly off in all directions. If not? Tell that person he or she needs a shower.

Happy Campers Canada
Order Confirmation # 98470948
One (1) Silva Explorer Compass
Date of order: March 10, 2016, 10:55 a.m.
Purchased by: M. Perkins
Shipping Address: Unit 9, 2975 Pine Grove Lane, Old Rat Creek, BC, V0N 2K8

Thank you for your recent order! The Silva Explorer Compass keeps you and your buddies on course while you are hiking, hunting or simply exploring. Two-degree gradations and declination scales make it easy for you to plot a precise path. This compass comes with a sturdy lanyard, so you can wear it around your neck to keep it within easy reach. Also included

is a magnifier, which makes this outdoor compass easy to read. We know you won't be disappointed with your purchase. Click here to order an altimeter at 15 per cent off!
Cost: $18.00
Delivery charge: $7.95 (ships in 7–9 business days).
Payment Method: VISA **** **** **** 1021, expiry date 09/18
"Go Play Outside!"

Email Message
From: Doug
To: Margery
March 13, 9:30 p.m.

I forgot to check before you left today about that Gaussmeter you were after. Did you mean one of those thingamabobs that measure magnetic flux density? The last time we had a request for a Gaussmeter was when those high school kids were having a seance and they thought they could detect paranormal energy. You going ghost busting?

Sent from my iPhone

The Donut Hole: Incident Report
Employee: Todd Hewson
Shift Manager: Ken Trunkle
March 14, 2016, 4:00 p.m. (approx.)

Two women seated at Table 12 (actually a booth) started doing this weird thing with spoons. I recognized them because they are regulars and also one of them goes to church with my mom. One lady was patting the other lady with spoons, all over her. Like, tapping her, slowly. Then she would kind of let go and the spoons were sticking on her, even when she stood up. Then they started doing it with forks too. And knives. Not the plastic takeout spoons either. The real ones. They must have had some kind of glue or invisible tape or it was a thing with static electricity. At one point there were approximately fifteen or twenty spoons and forks and knives on the one lady, hanging from her arms and legs and back and front and even on her face.

Naturally, I suspected they were going to steal them. Thinking of our meeting of last month re utensil loss, I told the shift manager (Ken) to come and check it out and he did. He said (and I quote) that was the most fucked-up-est thing he'd ever seen. Then he told me to do this incident report while he went over there and told the ladies to put the utensils back. They did. Then they left.

PS I said we should run them through the dishwasher but as usual no one took my advice.

The Weekly Ratter

TOURISM OUR ONLY HOPE, SAYS MAYOR

Local Economy in Steep Decline

Maya Ruth, Staff Writer

With five local businesses having closed their doors in the past 30 days, Old Rat Creek Mayor Vern Glasscock says the area needs tourist dollars to revitalize the economy and lift residents' spirits. He says bringing visitors to town is essential to re-establish a robust economy and save the businesses that remain.

Glasscock encourages residents to post "awesome pictures of how awesome our town can be" on social media. "We're living in a tourist-driven economy. Whistler's got their ski hill and what have you. Kelowna's got vineyards. But the people of Old Rat Creek are really friendly, and the scenery is awesome. The trees! The fields! The creek! We've just got to get the word out. Call your friends! Call your family! Tell 'em we're friendly! Tell 'em it's beautiful here!"

Chamber of Commerce and Tourism Board officials will be meeting next Wednesday (March 29) to discuss strategies for an economic enhancement plan. Public input is encouraged.

---

iPhone transcription of registered user M. Perkins
March 15, 2016, 3:09 p.m.
Apple Privacy Centre, Toronto, ON, Canada

Margery: Can a concussion cause body changes?
Siri: I'm not sure I understand.
Margery: Why do I feel a pull toward metal objects?
Siri: Interesting question.
Margery: I'm going crazy.
Siri: There's no need for that.
Margery: Do fat people attract metal?
Siri: Let's see. Here's what I found on the web for "Do fat people attract metal": "Are women attracted to fat men?" www.peertrainer.com; "Fat Bottomed Girls, heavy metal remix" www.bangyourhead.com; "Why do I attract fat people?" www.answers.yahoo.com
Margery: If I stay in bed all day will this condition go away?
Siri: Let's see. Here's what I found on the web for "If I stay in bed all day, will this condition go away?": "Why do depressed people lie in bed?" www.psychdoctor.com; "Bedrest: Does it help your condition?" www.mommieslife.com; "How to recover from sleeping all day." www.woeisme.org; "Get fired up in bed!" www.spiceitup.com

Margery: You are no help at all.
Siri: I do my best.
Margery: Maybe I do need a drink.
Siri: OK—check it out. Here's what I found on the web for licensed restaurants near you: The Woodcutter, 1436 Canoe Landing; Pony Bar and Grill, 65 Main Street.

Magic Mini Whiteboard Message
Mom,
Have you seen my saxophone? It's not in the case and I need it for band tomorrow.
Owen

*****TELUS** **11:31 PM** **38%**
Naomi

Still happening?

yup

So weird!

yup

Ever think it might be a sign from God?

nope

Seriously. Like people who get visions of Mother Mary on their toast. Or start bleeding from their hands. Like it's the wounds of Jesus from getting nailed to the cross.

Naomi, I have paper clips all over me.
Maybe it's a sign from Office Depot.

I don't think you're taking it seriously.

oh, I am taking it seriously. I'm seeing
Dr. Payne on Monday

Maybe it's a heavenly gift, and you are meant
to use it for good in the world. You should
pray for an answer.

How about you pray, I'll go see doc.

gnite.

God bless

The Weekly Ratter

Section B: Community Chatter!

LOCAL WOMAN SAVES DAY WITH MAGNETIC POWER

Grandpa can get back on his Harley

Maya Ruth, Staff Writer

When Jim Cole's father lost his motorcycle key on Monday, he thought he might be stuck in the BC Interior forever. He never dreamed that a human magnet would save the day.

But that's exactly what happened when Jim Cole Sr., who had stopped for a visit with his son's family while en route from Edmonton to Langley, dropped the key for his Harley-Davidson 2002 Sportster somewhere in West Hills Park picnic area during a family barbecue.

"That key was lost somewhere between the woods behind the outhouse and the parking lot," said the younger Cole. "It could have been in the grass, in the gravel, in the dirt. Anywhere! And he didn't have a spare."

The Coles had been searching for over an hour, when it seemed their prayers were answered.

"This woman was walking by and asked what we were doing. Well, when we told her we'd lost that key, she just took her Crocs off and slowly walked around the park and I'll be damned if the key didn't stick right to her foot. It was over in the weeds by the doggie-doo bag dispenser. She also found four dollars and twenty-five cents in loonies and quarters, a few bottle caps and one earring."

Jim Cole, Sr. was able to get to Langley on schedule. "Sure, I love visiting family in your town, but nobody likes to feel stranded," he said during a telephone interview. "Who knows how long we would have been out there on our hands and knees if that lady hadn't shown up. We invited her to stay for a hot dog but she said she was on her way to a doctor's appointment."

The woman's identity could not be confirmed.

Alexander Mackenzie High School physics and biology teacher John Stoddart said there is no such thing as a human with magnetic power. He said the woman likely had a metal detector hidden in the leg of her pants.

Email Message
From: Dr. E. Payne, GP
To: Dr. W. R. King, Endocrinologist
April 5, 1:43 p.m.

Margery Perkins ("Patient") is experiencing unnatural attraction to metal. (Tested in examining room 4D with coins, thumbtacks and a variety of steel diagnostic instruments.) Unprecedented in my clinical experience. No pain associated with attraction. Also presents mild asthma, tooth sensitivity, psoriasis on upper arms. Moderately obese. See attached blood tests.

Signed, by email
Dr. Emily Payne
Blue Sky Medical Centre

Magic Mini Whiteboard Message
Mom, where is all the change from my money jar? It was all replaced with fives and tens and twenties. And I found my sax in your room… since when do you play?
love Owen

Old Rat Creek Community Forum Facebook Post
April 19, 2016, 7:45 p.m.

To the lady who was crossing at the intersection of Frontier and Arbutus:

I am so sorry! This has never happened before. I didn't get a chance to apologize before you dashed off, but seriously it was as if my bike had a mind of its own. I came at you like there was a wind that blew me into you. I hope you're okay, and I want you to know that it wasn't my fault. Lucky for me my carbon-fibre frame wasn't damaged!

If our town planners thought about making a bike lane for non-emitting commuters, maybe this kind of accident wouldn't happen! Hello, Old Rat Creek town council?

Please share if you support cyclists!

April 23, 2016
From the desk of Dr. W. R. King,
Endocrinologist, North Vancouver, BC
Re: Margery Perkins, Old Rat Creek

Patient reports physical attraction toward iron, steel and mixed metals. No attraction reported toward aluminum.

Endocrine system within range, including adrenals, pituitary, pineal, thyroid, parathyroid.

Possible anemia.

Suggestion: Increase consumption of leafy greens, legumes, red meat.

Psychological assessment recommended.

Further testing required.

*****TELUS** **6:42 PM** **38%**
Naomi

Can I ask you a favour?

Of course

And as my BFF and former sponsor,
promise you won't think I'm weird?

I'm still your sponsor. Always will be. And I already think you're weird. What's up?

I'm having some issues
with my lower back.

Easy. Need a massage?

Not exactly.

Coins stuck where you can't reach again?

Ha ha.

I only put them in
reachable places now.

Good.

But I do need you to come over and
run an iron up and down my spine.

?

Don't have to plug it in.
Don't have to heat it up.
Just iron places I can't reach.
Hello?
Hello?

Ya, I can do that.

Thank you. It's kinda urgent.

OK. I'm bringing Pastor Kirk.

He really likes you.
And is totally non-judgmental.

Magic Mini Whiteboard Message
Dear Owen,
Oh yeah, sorry about the $$. I needed change for parking. Hope I left the correct amount in bills. You had seventy-five dollars in quarters, loonies and toonies in there! Great savings plan!
Love, Mom

Voicemail recording from 604-966-****
Hi Margery, it's me, Megan! We met on the Greyhound when you were going to your doctor's appointment a while back. Remember? Anywho, it was great to chat. Like I was saying, the mainstream medical industry doesn't always have our best interests at heart. That acupuncturist I was trying to remember is Dr. Jian Chen. He's the real deal. Helped me with my fibroids. Google C-H-E-N Acupuncture. You don't have to call me back. Good luck! Bye!

From the AA *Big Book*:
The Serenity Prayer
God grant me the serenity to accept the things I cannot change,
Courage to change the things I can,
And the wisdom to know the difference.

www.unclescottsMSFsupplies.com

UNCLE SCOTT'S MAGNETIC SHIELDING FOIL AND SUPPLIES

"America's Best Material Available for Shielding DC, ELF & VLF Magnetic Fields" …and great service too!

Industry experts have trusted Uncle Scott to shield delicate electronic components from EMFs for years! And now, this flexible magnetic shielding foil made of 80 per cent nickel alloy can be yours at affordable prices for your use at your home or business. Choose from thinner material that can be easily trimmed with ordinary kitchen scissors and shaped by hand, or our thicker material, which offers higher shielding performance (requires tin snips to cut. Click here to order).

Use our unique shielding foil to create a magnetic barrier for your doorbell transformer, cellphone, microwave oven, buried wiring and more. You can expect as much as 82 per cent attenuation of the magnetic field with one layer of shielding (providing the shield fits snugly). Multiple layers can be used for even greater reduction.

NOTE: We recommend using a Gaussmeter to determine the exact shape and positioning of the shielding foil, and to confirm that the magnetic fields have been reduced to desired levels.

CAUTION: shielding foil has sharp edges! Please use extreme caution when cutting.

Magnetic Shielding Foil: 15" wide, 0.003" thick (# N785-3) $27.95/linear ft [add to cart]

Magnetic Shielding Foil: 15" wide, 0.011" thick (# N785-4) $33.95/linear ft [add to cart]

Magic Mini Whiteboard Message

Mom, this town is SOOOOOO BORING AND DEAD. Me and Felix are thinking of moving to Vancouver after graduation.
Love, Owen

Email Message
From: Doug
To: Margery
May 10, 11:30 a.m.

Margery, this has got to stop. I don't care what you do in your spare time (you know that) but now it's starting to really affect your work. Norm saw you wrapping the grade 30 proof coil chain (with hot galvanized finish) around your waist and draping it over your shoulders in the break room yesterday. He thought it was some kind of bondage/S&M thing. People are starting to talk! Margery, you're not doing a very good job of "hiding" this so-called "affliction." I've told you time and time again to keep your hands out of the screws. It's bad enough when you are always pressing yourself against the shelving.
—D

Sent from my iPhone

*****TELUS** **7:22 PM** **64%**

Naomi

Can I come to church with you?

Of course!

Couldn't hurt to get a little direction I suppose.

God will be delighted to see a heathen like you ha ha. So will Pastor Kirk.

I'm not interested in the pastor, and I don't think God's interested in me.

"Do not fear, for I am with you. Do not be dismayed, for I am your God. I will strengthen you and help you; I will uphold you with my righteous right hand." (Isaiah, 41:10)

I got stuck to the side of a delivery van yesterday. Had to get Doug to pull me off.

I'll pick you up...

Thanks

Wait: do you mean for Sunday morning in the sanctuary, or Wednesday evening in the basement?

Ah, ye of little faith. Sunday!

See you at 9:45.

Jian Chen's Family Acupuncture Clinic
Richmond, BC
(private and confidential)

Memo to All Staff:

Due to the incident last month in our Cook Road clinic, treatment rooms will now be equipped with emergency pliers. Please remember that if a needle enters the tissue smoothly and without resistance, this indicates an energy meridian. However, if a needle appears to be *pulled* or *sucked* in any way *into* the body of a patient, the procedure must be stopped immediately and Dr. Chen must be alerted.

It is your responsibility to familiarize yourself with the use of the pliers.

Xiexie,
Mrs. Chen

Dear Ms. Perkins,

I, along with the members of the clergy here at Old Rat Creek Apostolic Church, would like to thank you for the unique offering-cum-special event after last Sunday's worship service in the sanctuary. When Naomi McFadden tossed that loonie at you and it stuck on your (lovely) dress, we all thought it was some kind of prank! We thought there must be some adhesive quality to the coin. But when the seniors put down their teacups and began rummaging through their wallets for change to toss at you, we knew that a Holy Presence had been delivered. Never has the congregation had such fun with their offerings!

Please accept my apologies for Mrs. Henry. At ninety-one years old, even though her hearing is just about gone, her throwing arm seems to get stronger and stronger. I hope the swelling in your forehead went down quickly.

I was delighted that the youngsters, who normally spend Community Sharing Time drinking juice and eating digestive biscuits and sliding around in their stocking feet downstairs, all came up to see what was going on. Of course, they asked their parents for money to toss. Praise God, indeed. Although unorthodox, it was certainly appreciated.

If you are so moved, I would be delighted to discuss making the Sunday Coin Toss a regular event at Old Rat Creek Apostolic Church.

Sincerely,
Pastor Kirk Bedrock

PS I hope you enjoyed my sermon on accepting miracles. How timely! That $182 will be put to good use in God's name.

PPS Ms. McFadden probably already told you, but it's Hip Hop Hallelujah next Friday here. Hope you can make it! Singles Mingle nights are really a gas.

Fortune from Peking Moon Express fortune cookie
A gift unopened is just a wrapped box.

Magic Mini Whiteboard Message
Dear Owen,
Moving? Vancouver?
Sure, Rat Creek's in a slump, but these things come and go.

Let's talk tomorrow.
Love, Mom
PS After our chat the other day, I am trying to see this thing between me and metal as a gift. Just have to figure out how to put it to good use. Just like you should do something amazing with your gift of playing soccer so well.
PPS there's leftover Chinese in the fridge

Facebook Messenger
Margery—I thought I'd send you this. Found it on www.youatewhat.com:

Top 10 Strange Cravings
1. Ice
2. Toothpaste
3. Coal
4. Sponges
5. Dirt
6. Chalk
7. Newspapers
8. Matches (cardboard, with sulphur tip)
9. Starch
10. Rubber (erasers, balloons, elastic bands) (tires excluded)

Other strange cravings that people reported include bricks, laundry soap and raw sausages.
Doesn't mean there's no one else in the world who craves metal and thinks about gulping down a ball bearing now and then. But I don't think it's safe. Lick it—sure. Don't see the harm, as long as it's clean. Swallow it? No. Don't do it. Just like before, if you feel the urges getting so strong you don't think you can fight them alone, call. I'm here for you.
—Naomi

Bird World Weekly
June 9, 2016

Thousands of migratory birds—including waterfowl (ducks and geese), raptors (hawks and eagles), wading birds (cranes, herons, gulls, terns and shorebirds), and songbirds (sparrows, warblers, blackbirds and thrushes)—known to be on their north-south migratory path have been observed by western Canadian ornithologists flying in east-west directions. Reports to the British Columbia Bird Observation Centre (BC-BOC) since mid-June suggest that V-formations, which normally would be headed to Canada's North, have been colliding with each other, lead-bird first, over a sparsely populated area of central British Columbia.

University of Victoria zoology professor Jeremy Pyck said that although surprisingly little is understood about the neural substrates which support migratory birds' extraordinary navigational ability, the planet's magnetic field appears to be the primary (but not sole) orientation cue.

"Migratory birds are genetically programmed to fly a certain direction, based on geomagnetic pull. They aren't like puppies. They don't just fly higgledy-piggledy. This east-west flight pattern we're observing in some areas of BC really is unprecedented and suggests a kind of migratory path confusion. These birds are lost."

Wild Canada spokesperson Amber Rainbow said the tar sands activity is to blame.

<June 10, 2016>
Private and confidential
Margery Perkins
Notice of Termination

Dear <Ms. Perkins>,

I am writing to inform you of the termination of your employment with <Old Rat Creek Hardware>.

During our meeting of May 9, 2016, you were advised that targets for <not walking around with metal hardware stuck to you> were not being met, and that <safety/conformity standards were being compromised>.

On May 21, you had a second meeting with me. Also present were Tim Arnaud (Light Fixtures), Hanna Point (Seasonal) and Norm Went (Lumber). You were advised that your overall <not being magnetic> had not improved to the level required. In that meeting you were issued with a final warning letter. This letter indicated that your employment may be terminated if the aforementioned issue did not improve by <insert date>.

We consider that your <not being magnetic> is still unsatisfactory and have decided to terminate your employment for failure to comply with standards of on-the-job expectations. Your employment will end immediately. In lieu of receiving two weeks' notice, you will be paid the sum of $<1,862.00>, which includes accrued entitlements and outstanding remuneration, up to and including your last day of employment.

Yours sincerely,
Mr. Douglas Armstrong,
Manager, Old Rat Creek Hardware
cc Marty Stye, Independent Hardware Inc., Head Office

Email message
From: Doug
To: Margery
June 10, 11:40 p.m.

Jeez M, I'm sorry about that letter but I had to put it in

writing to make it official for head office, and that was the only template we had on file. My hands are tied. Frankly, Margery, I'm concerned about you. I've kept you on through "rough patches" before, but this involves knives, drill bits and saws. Not only are you putting yourself at risk working here, but we'd be liable as a company if you—or anyone else—got hurt while on shift.

I know you explained how the stuff doesn't come at you pointy end first, but I DO worry. And now you're not even wearing the Crocs or rubber gloves or that neoprene wetsuit under your uniform like you did at first. It's affecting your ability to work. It's affecting relationships with co-workers. Norm thinks your body was replaced by aliens! (I don't know if he was joking or not. Remember his crop circle theories?) But you must admit, whatever's going on with you is pretty hard to explain scientifically.

In any case, it's affecting sales. Business here has slowed down enough as it is. Remember last month's Up with Hardware meeting, where we talked about how everyone has to go above and beyond with customer service? Well, sorry to say it, but no one wants to "pluck" a piece of hardware off of you. ("The hinge you're looking for is stuck to the underside of my arm" just doesn't cut it, Margery.)

This isn't "personal" and of course I will write you a formal letter of reference! I think you'd be great somewhere like a store that sells wool or something. Or wicker furniture. And, yes (sorry I didn't get back to you on this earlier), you can certainly order that magnetic shielding foil from Uncle Scott's through the store—I'll run it in through my personal account so you can still get a staff discount. I think that's a great step. Fashion yourself a little "suit of armour." I'll give you a call when it arrives.

Cheers,
—D

Magic Mini Whiteboard Message
Dear Mom,
I'm staying with Felix until exams are done and we can leave. Because the way you're acting now, it's worse than when you were a drunk. A spaghetti pot on your head? Hello? I don't care whether it's a disease, a choice or a "gift." I'm gonna get a normal job in a normal place like a normal person.
Owen

Old Rat Creek Police Department, Incident Report
Case #2016-295034
Incident Type: Exposure
Incident Date: 06/27/2016, 2:15 a.m.
Incident Address: 200 block Pine St.
Arrested: Margery L. Perkins
Age: 40
Sex: Female
Address: Unit 9, 2975 Pine Grove Lane, Old Rat Creek, BC
Suspect was arrested for: Lewd, Lascivious Behaviour in a Public Place.
Details: The ORCPD, with information obtained by reports from passersby, arrested Ms. Margery Perkins for lewd behaviour as she was curled inside a corrugated steel culvert (diameter 0.85 metres) near town hall, without clothing. When asked to explain herself, Ms. Perkins pressed her tongue against the culvert and began muttering. Her words were incomprehensible.
Ms. Perkins was released on two hundred dollars bail to the

custody of Pastor Kirk Bedrock, who brought her a blanket and promised to arrange some form of community service as restitution.

Notice to Quit
July 2, 2016

NOTICE TO: Margery Perkins, TENANT in possession and all others

TAKE NOTICE THAT:

1. Pursuant to a written lease (the "Lease") dated January 1, 2004, the Tenant holds possession of the premises described as: Unit 9, Shady Acres, 2975 Pine Grove Lane, Old Rat Creek, BC (the "Premises").

2. On June 22, 2016, during routine maintenance, it was discovered that the Tenant had

   a. removed door from refrigerator in unit, and placed it on the bedroom floor. A foul odour emanated from the food remaining on the fridge shelves.
   b. accumulated a substantial number of landscaping tools and items from the Caretaker's Shed (including but not limited to: spades, rakes, trowels and large steel hedge trimmer).

3. Between June 3 and June 22, 2016, the Landlord received no less than twelve (12) complaints from Shady Acres residents about the Tenant's behaviour. Complaints include but are not limited to

   a. sprawling over the hoods of various parked cars in the (common) Parking Area,

b. climbing on the metal gate in the (common) Courtyard Area, and
c. physically blocking Mail Box access in the (common) Foyer.

4. Due to said damages and/or actions by the Tenant and/or the Tenant's guests, the Landlord hereby elects to terminate the Lease. The Tenant is given at least thirty (30) days' notice to quit the premises in compliance with the applicable laws in the province of British Columbia. Accordingly, the Tenant must vacate and surrender the Premises to the Landlord by noon on August 2, 2016.

THIS NOTICE TO QUIT IS GIVEN PURSUANT TO THE APPLICABLE LAWS OF THE PROVINCE OF BRITISH COLUMBIA AND IN NO WAY IMPAIRS OR LIMITS ANY OF THE OTHER REMEDIES OR RIGHTS THAT THE LANDLORD MAY HAVE UNDER THE LEASE OR UNDER SAID LAWS.

---

iPhone transcription of registered user M. Perkins
July 2, 2016, 3:49 p.m.
Apple Privacy Centre, Toronto, ON, Canada

Margery: Why is this happening to me?
Siri: Interesting question. Here's what I found on the web for "Why is this happening to me?": "Simple ways to reduce failure and increase positive energy" www.whyisthishappening.net; "Free Audiobook" www.whyme.org
Margery: Is this one of those things I can't change?
Siri: Okay. I found this on the web for "Is this one of those things I can't change?": "The wheel of change moves on, and those who were up go down and those..." www.quoted.com;

"15 Things You Can Do Today to Make a Positive Change" www.thechangeinyou.com
Margery: Is a large pile of metal a tourist attraction?
Siri: Here's what I found on the web for "Is a large pile of metal a tourist attraction?": "World's largest metal scarecrow, Minnesota" www.roadsidewonders.com; "20 Best Canadian Roadside Attractions: #1 The Ginormous Hockey Stick and Puck in Duncan, BC" www.mightybigstick.ca; "A Pile of Nuclear Waste Now a Tourist Attraction in Weldon Springs" www.amusingplanet.com

---

OLD RAT CREEK BUY, SELL, TRADE ANYTHING
Facebook Post
Closed Group

For Sale: Magnetic Shielding Foil, 15" wide, 0.011" thick.
Price: This is a steal at $10 OBO.
Details: Great for protecting sensitive electronic equipment from magnetic fields. You can use it to get rid of magnetic impulses. Don't need it anymore.
BONUS: I'll throw in a (gently) used Gaussmeter (device for detecting electromagnetic radiation. Also used in seances and for detecting paranormal activity.)
Contact: PM Margery if interested!

Voice mail recording from 604-894-****
Hey, kiddo, it's me, Mom. So, how's Vancouver? You and Felix gonna get tickets to one of those Whitecaps games? I miss you. I miss your messages on your silly old magic mini whiteboard. You know we've had that thing since you were three years old? I haven't erased your last one, where you

said you'd try to come back and visit. I sure hope you will. It's weird around here without you. Quiet. I guess I'm an empty nester now. Well, take care.

Travel BC: August eNews
Odd Roadside Attractions for the Whole Family
Here's one roadside attraction you're sure to be attracted to! Something amazing has popped up in the quaint little town of Old Rat Creek (Exit 5 off Highway 72). Travellers of all ages will love "Magnetic Margery," a dazzling eleven-foot tower of metal objects.

You, too, can join the fun by adding something metal to Magnetic Margery! Hey, son, why not add a little metal hot rod toy car? Maybe sis wants to toss on a piece of loonie store jewellery! Mom and Dad can contribute a safety pin, a bottle cap or a fishing lure! Let's watch the tower grow and grow as metal pieces cling to it.

Local legend has it that tossing something metallic at Magnetic Margery will bring good luck. Just like tossing coins in a fountain or making a wish on a falling star! People come from far and wide to add their metal pieces to this one-of-a-kind tower.

Located in BC Pioneer Heritage Park, at the intersection of Main Street and Second Avenue (beside the Esso). See map below.

Warning: Visitors with artificial cardiac pacemakers are advised to stay at least three metres from the tower (behind the yellow line). The town of Old Rat Creek is not responsible for the loss of keys, coins, metal eyeglasses or other valuables to the tower. Metal objects you do not wish to add to Magnetic Margery should be held securely.

* *The Magnetic Margery Roadside Attraction is patrolled by AA Aardvark Security twenty-four hours a day.*

Old Rat Creek Tourism Bureau
Private Memo to Board of Directors
August 17, 2016

CONFIDENTIAL

Volunteers are still needed to administer Margery's noon smoothie meal replacement through the plastic feeding tube. Thanks to Amelia and Josh, who have tended to her for the past six weeks, to Dr. Louis, who designed her evacuation trough, and to the Green Hippie for providing a different flavour of organic, high-protein meal replacement smoothie for Margery every day.

CBC News
October 14, 2016
Old Rat Creek Becomes New BC Tourist Mecca
A new hot spot has emerged on the western Canadian tourist scene. Visitors to Old Rat Creek, BC, have made this sleepy little town, two hundred kilometres from the nearest mall, the "Place to Be," according to Tourism BC. Visitor numbers from the period between the August long weekend (BC Day) and Thanksgiving (October 11) indicate approximately 31,900 people made the trip up Highway 72 to Old Rat Creek, putting the destination fourth (after Whistler, Tofino and the Okanagan) for tourist visits.

The spike in visitors is due to the town's giant metallic "wishing tower" dubbed "Magnetic Margery." According to local lore, an unemployed, homeless, overweight, introverted single mother who suffers from alcoholism and psoriasis lives inside the tower and pulls the metal objects toward her with a magnetic force bestowed upon her by God.

Old Rat Creek Apostolic Church Pastor Kirk Bedrock

said tourists have not only been tossing their metal objects at Magnetic Margery, they've been filling the pews every Sunday. "We haven't had attendance like this since the Canucks made the playoffs," he said. "But all kidding aside, I think we have a modern-day miracle here."

FOR IMMEDIATE RELEASE
2017 Spring/Summer Job Fair
(Sponsored by the Old Rat Creek Economic Development Department)

Come one, come all, and learn about all the employment opportunities in our booming town! Skilled and unskilled workers needed. Bring your resumé and bring your friends. Interviews may be conducted on the spot. Booths will be set up at the town office on Saturday, May 5, from 9:00 a.m. to 9:00 p.m. with HR representatives from the following companies:

- Ye Olde Rat Creeke Fudgery
- Old Rat Creek Best Western
- Owen and Felix's "Whitecaps North" Indoor Soccer Training Academy
- Oh Canada, Eh? Maple Syrup and T-Shirts Retail Emporium
- Naomi's Next-to-Godliness Soap Company
- True North Performing Arts Centre
- Tim Hortons (formerly The Donut Hole)
- Canadian Tire (formerly Old Rat Creek Hardware)

And many more! The band Iron Glory (formerly Satan's Ballsack) will be playing gospel rock in the foyer of the town office all afternoon.

Old Rat Creek Community Forum Facebook Post
June 1, 2017, 10:55 p.m.

—Did anybody see that lightning? OMG, it was right over the Wishing Tower!
—That's the kind of bolt God usually saves for Saskatchewan
—Well, duh, metal attracts lightning. You people are such idiots.
—Crazy. I don't even see clouds.

The Daily Ratter
06/02/2017
LIGHTNING HITS TOURIST ATTRACTION
Mona Ruth, Editor
A bolt of lightning struck the top of Magnetic Margery just before eleven last night, apparently causing Old Rat Creek's version of the Eiffel Tower to lose its magnetic quality and come crashing down. No one was injured on the outside of the tower. Emergency crews are searching for the body of Margery Perkins, whom one Chamber of Commerce official, on the condition of anonymity, claims lived within the tower.

The public is being advised to stay away from the area until further notice.

Old Rat Creek Tourism Bureau
Private Memo to Board of Directors
June 2, 2017
CONFIDENTIAL

Although rumours abound, we can confirm that the fire department, the ambulance and the police, along with Happy

Scrappy's Metal Recyclers and Bob the Welder Welding Services, were unable to find any human remains within the pile of metal debris at Heritage Park. The investigation will continue. CBC, Global, CTV and CNN are covering the story. Don't forget what they say: all publicity is good publicity. And as Tourism Bureau Chair Kirk Bedrock says, "Think of what happened to religion when Jesus died!"

Don't forget, tonight is opening night for the new production at True North Performing Arts Centre (*Pine Beetle: The Musical*).

---

www.geomagneticphenomenon.ca

According to the Canadian Space Weather Forecast Centre (CSWFC), unprecedented levels of aurora borealis (northern lights) have been visible over central British Columbia recently. Forecasters are uncertain as to why this phenomenon is occurring; there has been no significant change in geomagnetic activity (solar flares). Waves of green and purple were first reported on June 4 (23:10), and have been visible to the naked eye, even during daytime hours, since the initial observations.

Auroral activity is typically produced by the ionization and excitation of atmospheric elements (charged particles) in the magnetosphere, which then become luminescent. Lucien Valencia, a spokesperson for the International Association of Oceanic and Atmospheric Research said that, though unlikely, geomagnetic forces escaping an object, organism or geological feature on the top layer of the earth's surface (the crust) could explain the abnormally intense display of cosmic hue.

Satellite images and individual sighting reports indicate the unnaturally intense cosmic phenomena appears to be strongest near the town of Old Rat Creek, where a freak lightning bolt caused irreparable damage to a local landmark exactly three days prior to the appearance of the aurora borealis.

Delighted town officials reported that power grids, radio communication and GPS systems in the area are working "better than ever," and they are mounting a campaign to rebrand their town as Northern Lights Capital of the World.

Western Canadian Aurora Borealis Tracker Facebook Group (Public)

Becky posted a video from Old Rat Creek, BC, June 4, 2017
138,308 views
9387 comments

—Holy crap! Great vid Becky!
—I've never seen blues and greens and pinks like that EVER. Even when I was cross-country skiing in the Arctic Circle. This place is amazing.
—People. Wake up. Global warming brings on more intense aurora. Stop Big Oil now before this becomes our new normal.
—Anyone see the V of geese flying through the northern lights? Anyone? Pretty freakin cool.
—I got a used Gaussmeter a few months ago. As soon as those northern lights appeared, it started beeping like nuts all day.
—OMG, the sky was so bright and dazzling through the window my granddaughter couldn't fall asleep.
—So? Close the curtain old lady!
—We don't have those brilliant lights so strong even here in Iceland.
—Like God's favourite crayons were melting.

Mycology

J.J., the station manager at CHXL, invited Nick Price to take a seat in his office. Offered him a gummy bear—or gummy snake? gummy shark?—from a clear plastic bag with the outline of a clown on the front. Nick politely refused. With his dental history, he didn't dare. They discussed hockey, road construction near the station, someone's new motorcycle. J.J. asked Nick his opinion of a new band that had released a single on SoundCloud. Nick had never heard of them, but told J.J. he thought they were hot. Super hot. The next big thing.

The twerp probably knew he was lying. It had probably been a set-up.

J.J. stuffed the candy bag in his desk drawer, started nervously straightening out a paper clip, lowered his voice. He blinked excessively when he looked at Nick. "You know, Price, I bet you'd be a whole hell of a lot happier if you had time to play a little more golf." He twisted his mouth, popped a finger inside and picked some chewed gummy from his back molars. He frowned at it, then wiped it under his desk.

"Sorry, did you say golf?" said Nick.

"Yeah! That's right, golf. Wouldn't it be great to hit the links when it's not crowded? Like a Tuesday afternoon. Or a Thursday morning. Whenever you'd like."

"J.J., you know I don't play golf. And who said I was unhappy? What are you talking about?"

"I'm talking about freedom, Price. Some leisure time. You deserve it." J.J. lifted both arms in the air like he was running through some marathon finish-line tape. That's when it hit Nick. He knew exactly what his boss was talking about. J.J. brought his arms down, unzipped his hoodie and poked the straight-as-a-pin paper clip into the soil of a bamboo plant on his desk. He said that Nick had been a loyal, punctual and hard-working employee for such a long time, and he hated to say it but the world was changing and Nick didn't seem to connect with the new market. He said new listeners had so many choices. Everyone at the station needed to stay relevant. And hungry. Then he opened an iPad and clicked on a chart with Nick's sales figures.

J.J. didn't have a family. He had a twenty-one-year-old vegan girlfriend with a diploma in crisis management.

Nick had invented the yellow and blue sticker with the radio station's call numbers that loyal listeners used to put on the back windows of their cars.

J.J. didn't have a land line.

Nick didn't have Snapchat.

"You mean I'm too old for this station. Is that it?"

"That's not what I said."

"It's what you meant."

"Think of the precious time you could spend with your grandchildren."

Nick didn't have grandchildren. He stood up, straightened his tie and thanked J.J. for his time. His face was hot and the briefcase in his hand felt ridiculous.

"Hang on," said J.J. "Don't you want to hear about the severance package?"

The shower curtain hanging in the only bathroom at the Prices' home was made of opaque brown plastic. Nick tucked it inside the bathtub so water wouldn't spray onto the tile floor.

He'd barely adjusted the water temperature when Shera came in.

"You're home early," his wife said. She didn't wait for an explanation, thankfully. "I swear to God, your mother has the thermostat set to one thousand degrees." Nick heard her run the sink and splash water on her face.

He knew he didn't fit in with the others at the station anymore. He was the last of the originals, from when they first hit the airwaves back in the eighties, and now that made him an outsider. He didn't laugh at their jokes, didn't go for beers with them after work. They shaved their chest hair but grew their beards. He wasn't interested in their weekend rock-climbing trips. They spent their money on titanium road bikes and tattoos. He spent his money on insurance, his daughter's lacrosse fees, car repairs and dentures for his mother. They saw him as a relic. Maybe they were right. Deadwood. A vestigial organ of the old station. He was just cluttering things up.

He put on the exfoliating shower gloves, poured some liquid soap into one palm and rubbed his hands together to work up a lather. Eyes shut, he stroked the hair on his belly upwards, against the grain. The tug felt uncomfortable in a good way. Like pulling off a tight woollen toque, being licked by a cat.

"You have no idea how lucky you are, being a man," said Shera through the Sensodyne froth. She brushed her teeth after everything she ate, always so aggressively it sounded like someone scraping burnt hamburger off the barbecue grill. "You never have to worry about hormones. You never have to worry about anything."

They had been married long enough for Nick to know she didn't expect a response. Certainly not a solution or a suggestion, or worst of all, a change of topic or a one-up. It would come out sooner or later. *Well, there is one little thing I have to worry about,* he could say. *My life. Oh, and also my future. And my purpose. But hey, it's okay! There's a real demand for tired old men with outdated sales skills. They'll be lining up to hire me. I might even get headhunted.*

He heard her spit, rinse the toothbrush, tap it twice on the edge of the sink, chuck it back in the Mason jar. "Love you," she said, and closed the door behind her, not gently.

It was difficult to breathe when he bent over, but he managed to reach his feet to give them a scrub. His toenails were the colour of peanut shells and the skin was cracked like dry clay around his heels, even when wet. The water on the shower floor became grey.

In two weeks, they'd celebrate their twenty-fifth wedding anniversary. He knew there was no need to hide from her that he'd been fired. Laid off. Let go. Whatever. That he was now unemployed. She'd be compassionate; she always was. *Maybe it's a blessing,* she'd say. *You've talked about getting out of radio ad sales for so long. Now's your chance to try something new. The house is paid off, and we can get by on my income as a nurse, no problem. We could travel. You could go back to school. See it as an opportunity!*

This attitude of hers could drive a man mad.

Nick squirted more soap onto his shower gloves and worked them around his crotch. He pulled his testicles to one side, then the other. Gave them a half-hearted jostle. It had been weeks—maybe over a month?—since they'd made love. When the night sweats came and she kicked the duvet off and flopped around the bed like a fish at the bottom of a boat, he knew better than to touch her. So he touched himself.

It was true he didn't feel passionate about the radio station anymore. He didn't even listen to it in the car on the way home from work. He didn't care for the DJs' banter or the music they played. Even the ads he'd sold and helped produce, he couldn't bear.

The bathroom door opened again. "Don't mind me, Dad." There was a click and a creak and Nick knew Emma was rifling through the bottom cupboard where they kept the tampons. He prayed she was just grabbing one out of the box to pop into her purse. She wouldn't actually put one in while he was there, would she? He quickly blocked the thought of his daughter and menstrual cycles and inserting tampons and blood with an image of her in their backyard, hair matted from never being brushed, wearing a fuzzy tiger-striped one-piece pyjama suit with plastic feet, cutting the grass with tiny scissors and tossing it into a salad bowl.

Nick started whistling so Emma wouldn't think that he was thinking about her having her period. It was the radio station's theme song—the only tune he ever whistled. The song he'd helped write, back in the day.

"I'm taking the bus to Malcolm's," said this thirteen-year-old girl, woman, stranger. "Then he's going to drive me to lacrosse." Nick would take preschool Emma to watch the older girls play lacrosse; he clearly remembered hoisting her onto his shoulders so she'd have a better view, and feeling her wet, sticky ice cream hands grasping his hair.

"Okay," he said. "Have fun."

Then, wait. *What?* "Just a minute, Em. Who's Malcolm? And how is he old enough to drive?" He pulled the shower curtain open enough to interrogate her, and to see what she was wearing and whether he needed to police it. But she was gone. The bathroom door was wide open.

Nick pulled the curtain closed again and let the water embrace him.

He resumed the ritual cleaning and bored fondling between his legs. *Not relevant. New markets.* He went back to his testicles. The old brother-plums were warm, tired and familiar.

He'd been in radio since he was barely out of college, even though his lisp meant he would never sit behind the microphone. He'd invented the station's *Caught Ya Listening!* campaign, where they'd award prize packages to people who were caught with the radio dial tuned to 1150. Thirty-five goddamn years. Thrown into a compost heap.

Nick's face wasn't the one on the bus shelters. He wasn't the "personality" being called upon to emcee charity events and flip pancakes at fundraising breakfasts. But it was Nick who brought in the ad revenue and promotional sponsorship that made the station tick. He sold airtime. Air and time: Shera used to joke that only the devil and a radio ad sales manager could make a living selling people air and time.

And then he felt it.

Something, between his legs. Above the base of his penis, and slightly off to the right. Something that didn't belong there. He looked down, afraid to exhale. Within the dark, shadowy pubic forest, there was a small protrusion. A fleshy bulb. Nick felt a sour taste in the back of his throat. The thing was attached to him. His mind jumped to the king of maladies. At his age, he automatically thought every new freckle or bump must be cancer. He took the scratchy gloves off so he could investigate it with his bare fingertips. The thing didn't feel like he'd imagined a tumour to feel. It wiggled slightly, then returned to attention. He pulled on it gently, and the skin around it tugged. The protrusion was fleshy, but it was not *his* flesh. What the hell was it? Narrow at the bottom, a thin stalk and on top a tiny cup, a bell shape.

He pinched it, bent it a little, then a little more, and with a crisp, horrifying snap, the thing came off painlessly between his fingers. He let out a squeal, then brought it into the light to examine it. The growth mocked him by being sort of cute, the way a worm or an earwig or a scurrying purple shore crab is cute when you flip over a rock on the beach and realize that life secretly exists in even the small, dark, moist places. He didn't know much about oncology, but something told him it wasn't cancer. You can't pluck off the Big C.

A sudden splash and the lapping of water broke Nick's focus. The shower curtain punched inward at his knees. He yanked it back to see Eleanor Rigby, her front paws on the toilet seat and her head in the bowl, slurping the cold contents. Her wagging tail hit the shower curtain a few more times, then the blue heeler–German shepherd mix looked at him lovingly and started licking water from the edge of the tub.

"Hey! Am-scray. Get lost, mutt."

The dog heaved a sad sigh and flopped onto the bath mat. Nick held the snapped-off thing at eye level, with arms stretched long so he could see it clearly without his glasses. Water bounced off its smooth, bruise-coloured surface, rinsing away soap suds and stray pubic hairs. He blew on it, perhaps to make the thing magically become something else; a precious gem that he could give to his wife, or a dove that would fly away. Yet the thing remained. Its simple forest quality was undeniable.

Nick had sprouted a mushroom.

A three-centimetre-ish bit of fungal matter. A living organism, erupted from his flesh. He squinted and tried to think of…

The door burst open.

"Hey, Dad. I'm gonna need some money." Emma was back.

Nick held the tiny mushroom—toadstool? No, too terrible of a word—in one hand; the other hand was feeling around the place in his public hair where he'd picked it. There was a little stump. It felt like what he imaged an umbilical cord root would feel like. Essentially, it was a hard outie.

Louder: "Helloooo? Earth to Dad."

There was no pain around the stump. When he pressed his ring finger on it, it felt like pressing on a scab, or on scar tissue.

"Twenty bucks, okay? I can pay you back after babysitting tomorrow."

No sensation on the top, but pressure underneath. A root.

"Or actually, forty. Forty would probably be good."

I am a log. A log in a forest. A felled log in a forest with a mushroom on it.

"There's a fifty here in your pants pocket. I'll just take that."

Nurse log. That's what it was called. A fallen tree, decaying. Dead, but providing a necessary home and nutrients for other life. Insects, lichen, moss. Mushrooms. *Relevant? Hungry? Necessary? I'll tell you about relevant.*

He suddenly felt itchy, and turned the shower head to "pulse."

Someone else came in.

"Budge over, kiddo, I gotta get my stretch-mark cream," said Greta, Nick's youngest cousin, twenty-two and very pregnant.

"You look even fatter today than yesterday!" said Emma.

"And you look uglier."

"You're like one of those exercise balls some of the fidgety kids sit on in class. Only bigger."

"Make yourself useful and rub some cream on my belly, 'kay?"

"Okaaaaay..."

"Sit on the toilet and you'll be just the right height. Warm it up in your hands first. Otherwise it'll shock the baby."

Nick knew that some people developed odd fungal infections. In fact, wasn't athlete's foot a fungus? But he'd had athlete's foot before. This was nothing like it. He could ask Shera. She'd know what it was. But even though she'd seen some of the most unusual medical conditions in her career, he could never talk to her about this. Never.

He raked his fingers through his pubic bush again, then through the hair under his arms. He stopped. There was another growth in the cavern of his left armpit. This one was smaller than the first, but with the same unmistakable shape. He gritted his teeth as if it might hurt, then pinched it and snapped it off. There was no pain. No bleeding. His daughter was rubbing cream on his pregnant cousin's belly, and he was harvesting mushrooms from his dark, hairy areas and rolling them between his fingers like they were foam earplugs.

"You know, you could take that into the kitchen," he said through the shower curtain. "Some privacy while a guy's taking a shower?"

They ignored him.

"What do you think it's going to be?" asked Emma. "Boy or girl?"

Technically, it's a parasite, thought Nick. *An organism living off another organism. An opportunist. A mooch.*

"A girl," said Greta. "Rub some down under my belly button. At the sides. Jesus! Your hands are cold! That's it. Yeah, for sure it's a girl."

"How do you know? How can you say for sure? Did you see the X-ray?"

"It's not an X-ray. It's an ultrasound. And I don't need to. I can read the baby's mind. And she's thinking girl thoughts."

"Like what kind of girl thoughts?"

"Like, 'Get me the hell out of here. I've got shit to do!'"

"What's this dark line of hair going down from your belly button?"

"That's normal."

"It doesn't look normal."

"It grows like that when you're pregnant."

"It's weird."

"You're weird."

Emma suddenly gasped and shrieked. "Oh my God! It kicked!" Eleanor Rigby barked at the sudden commotion.

"She does that all the time. Isn't it amazing?"

"If you really want to know, it's quite gross. All of it. I'm never having a baby. That's for sure."

The two left, arguing. The dog followed, the door slammed and Nick's mind plummeted.

What was wrong with him? How could this be? His body had secrets, and he felt betrayed. Invaded. Had he been exposed to spores somehow? He hadn't been in the woods for months. Hadn't been cooking with mushrooms. Hadn't even eaten any recently. It's not that he didn't like mushrooms—oyster, portobello, even shiitake and morels—alongside a steak or in stir-fry, but he was no expert. His mother had always dumped a tin of pre-sliced Money's mushrooms in the spaghetti sauce. She bought the dented tins for half price. They were the colour of elastic bands and felt like slippery erasers in his mouth. She didn't trust mushrooms that didn't come from a can.

The bathroom door opened, again. He heard the toilet seat flip up and the zip of a fly being pulled down. "Don't mind me, man." It was Bradley, the father-to-be, also living in the Prices' small home.

"I got a question for you," he said over the stream of urine and shower. "It's kinda personal, but when Shera had Emma, did you go watch? Like in the delivery room? I mean, I know you were there and all, at the hospital, but did you see everything, like, baby, placenta, all that shit coming out?"

"Yup," said Nick.

Nick heard the lurching stop-start-stop of Bradley's pee. He thought of the "fairy ring" of mushrooms that occasionally sprung up on the lawn.

"I wanna be there the whole time too. Like, it's the right thing to do—especially after all those prenatal classes me and Greta went to together—but I'm just feeling a little, you know, squeamish I guess would be the right word. I mean, miracle, yes, but also, *ew*, right? It wasn't, like, a massive turnoff, was it?"

Nick touched one of the mushrooms to his bottom lip. Felt its soft flesh, silky smooth. Like a newborn's toes.

"Nope," he said. "Not at all."

Then he took a little nibble of one of the mushrooms. It had the earthy taste of a raw potato, without the crunch. He felt a little guilty, like he did when he chewed on his fingernails or tasted the sweet mucous that dripped from his nose. Like when he masturbated.

"Good to know, man," said Bradley. There was a zip and a buckling up. "'Cause it's all pretty weird. I don't want to fail her. But, I mean: a baby? A living, breathing, thinking thing? Curled up inside her? Jesus Christ. It's like, *life*. Know what I mean?"

Nick chewed the tiny chunk of mushroom between his front teeth, like a morsel of food that might be too spicy, or too cold. Something told him not to swallow it. Why not? Was he afraid it was poisonous? He dabbed the mangled chunk from his tongue with his finger. If it was poisonous, wouldn't it have already killed him? If it was magic, wouldn't he already be high?

"Thanks for the pep talk, Nick. It's good to have a guy to vent to. Someone old, who's been through it."

"Right."

"Not that you're old-old, but, just, you know, *your* age."

"It's okay. I am old-old."

Nick thought of J.J.'s gummy bear as water washed the piece of mushroom off his fingertip, onto the shower floor. He used his big toe to squish it down the drain, then cleared his throat.

"Bradley, I have a question for you. Do you ever listen to the radio? Do you ever listen to my station?"

But Bradley was gone. There hadn't been a flush.

Maybe it was in his perspective. Perhaps this was a blessing, not a curse. Maybe the mushrooms were like little children of earth, and his aging body was the conduit for a heavenly miracle. He flipped the larger one over in his palm. Its delicate gills reminded him of a pleated summer sundress Shera had worn to a wedding they'd gone to the year before Emma had been born. They'd left the reception before the dancing had begun, inspired by the speeches and the champagne and the kissing, and walked all the way to the Meadow Lane Inn hand in hand, and made love. They didn't see the bride and groom again until after the honeymoon.

Had the mushrooms been inside him back them? Had he always been a carrier? Was having mushrooms like herpes, and he was only just now having an outbreak? These two had been hidden in forests of curly hair, but what if the next one grew from the palm of his hand? Sprouted from his thigh? His forehead? Was there a cure for mushrooms? Would he be prescribed fungicide? Were they contagious?

"Hey. Planning to save some water for the rest of the world?"

It was his mother. She was rummaging through a drawer.

He knew that the tiny snowy inkcap mushroom, with its beige cap and thin stem, like a floor lamp in a gnome house, grew best on horse manure. Did this mean his insides had completely gone to shit? Perhaps he was dying, and the mushrooms were warning signs, like yellow feathers left by canaries on their way out of the coal mine. Get your affairs in order. Prepare to be returned to the earth.

"You deaf?"

He pictured his own dead body, lying in a coffin, moss in his eye sockets, termites and maggots making a sponge of his flesh, mushrooms exploding from his mouth, his nose, ears, everywhere. Why bother with a coffin? Just lay him down in the forest. Decomposition is an impatient season.

"Or just ignoring me?"

"I won't be in the shower much longer, Ma." His voice quivered. "Do you think you can wait?"

"No. For heaven's sake, Nicholas, I definitely cannot wait. Don't be so selfish. You are not the king of France. My friends are coming over any moment. I need my lipstick. And my rouge."

Nick knew there were no friends coming over. She was eighty-nine, with dementia that kept her preening for visitors who never arrived.

"I can't let them see me like this. I won't. You don't know what they're like. They're judgmental old bitches. Especially that Meredith."

He peeked around the shower curtain and wondered if his mother could even see herself in the foggy mirror as she drew thick, dark lines where her eyebrows used to be. The charcoal pencil shook in her talon-like fingers. But there was an elegance to her, a dignity and pride despite everything.

"You look beautiful," said Nick. He recognized his daughter's angular jawline tucked within his mother's jowls. "Meredith will be jealous." His mother raised her hands to her throat and stroked the pearls that lay against her mottled, folded skin.

"Why, thank you," she said, holding her head as if there was a textbook balanced on top. She blotted her lips and the stain on the square of toilet paper was red as blood.

"Who's Meredith?"

Nick let it go.

"Now hurry and finish up in there," she said. "You'll be needed to make martinis downstairs for the guests."

"Sure. Why don't you go put on some music in the meantime?"

He knew she wouldn't remember what she was planning to do by the time she reached the end of the hall, but at least she closed the bathroom door gently when she left. He was finally in the bathroom alone with his auto-generated vegetable matter. He sniffed them; they smelled like lavender body wash.

Sixth caller through this morning gets a couple of surprise growths on their body! They're terrific fried up in garlic butter, served with a little salt and pepper! Now, back to Dan the Man's Top Thirty Countdown.

He pulled the shower curtain back, dropped both mushrooms into the yellow toilet water, and flushed. As they spun down, Nick thought of J.J.'s big, stupid beard, and wondered what was hiding in there. Perhaps all men had mushrooms, but no one spoke of them. The thought cheered him momentarily, then made him wish he had a brother.

The shower water went cold as the toilet bowl refilled. Nick dialled the setting from "pulse" to "standard spray" and let the chilly flow sting his chest. He touched the stump near his penis and the one in his armpit, and wondered if they'd grow back. Now that he didn't have a job, he could spend his time waiting for their return. It wasn't like there was anything better to do.

He had a friend who'd been laid off from his job as an insurance adjuster and still showered and got dressed in a suit and tie for work every day. Larry took the crowded morning bus downtown and sat in Tim Hortons watching daytime TV or playing solitaire on his phone, then took the five o'clock bus home at the end of the day. Like a dead tree that refused to fall to the forest floor. His wife had no idea. Or maybe she did. Maybe she was just playing along to save Larry the embarrassment.

Maybe these weren't Nick's first mushrooms. Maybe there'd been tiny clusters growing on Nick for months and he'd sloughed them off without noticing. Maybe Shera already knew; maybe she'd found them in his laundry or in the folds of the duvet in the morning and not said anything—to save him the embarrassment.

Nick opened his mouth. Water flooded in. He moved his tongue around, and it touched something meaty and smooth. *Holy shit.* Another fungal protrusion, this one growing from the inside of his cheek and nestled against his gums above his back molars. Smaller than the others, tucked up like a baby shrimp, or a gummy bear, in a place where it could hide and not be chewed. How long had it been there? He reached his fingers back, but instead of pinching it, he decided that this one, he would not pluck. This one he'd let be. He would be a gracious host to this curious guest. He'd gently flip the rock back over and let the quiet inhabitants of the dark, humid world stay hidden. He turned off the water, reached for a towel and patted himself, leaving some parts moist, wrapped the towel around his waist, and opened the curtain.

Shera was leaning against the counter brushing her long grey hair.

"You!" Nick hadn't heard her come in.

"Yup, me," she said, scanning his semi-nude body. "And, you." She was wearing loose, cropped pants. Varicose veins twisted like clematis vines around each calf and up her lower legs beneath the surface of her pale skin, thick and dark and intricate. Her toenails were painted the colour of the poisonous fly amanita. His tongue flicked the mushroom cap at the back of his mouth. Shera smiled.

"I was thinking the same thing," she said.

"Sorry?"

"I know, Babe. It's been way too long." She put down the brush and pulled the T-shirt over her head. Curly silver hair fell across her bare shoulders. Her skin glistened in the humidity.

"You're all steamy and clean. Irresistible." Shera had gained weight over the years; they both had. Her bra was too tight, cutting into her flesh like rubber bands on marshmallows, and her belly button was a deep cavern hidden between perfect fleshy drapes. Nick had been waiting for weeks for her to initiate intimacy—maybe months—but now he felt they needed to talk first.

"Wait, Sher. I've got something to tell... there's—I've..." he stammered. *How does one begin?* She put her index finger against his lips, shushing him.

"It's okay," she said, pressing one hand against the bathroom doorknob and twisting to lock it. She spider-walked her fingers through the hair on his chest, and he felt his heat rise, his face redden, the arches of his feet lift ever so slightly. Her hand reached a nub (fortunately, a nipple), which she took between her thumb and forefinger and twisted, at first gently, then as if she were unscrewing the lid off a tiny glass bottle of perfume. His eyes drifted up and their lids dropped down. He inhaled sharply through his nose and shuddered.

"Be still," she whispered playfully. "Quiet. Just stand there. Like a rock. Like a log. Don't move a muscle." She squeezed his other nipple, then she slowly untucked the corner of the towel from around his waist. It dropped to the floor. He parted his lips to speak and she silenced him by pressing her mouth on his and kissing him like she always did, forcefully at first, then pulling back slightly and gently biting his lower lip until her tongue could not resist exploring his lips, teeth, even his palate, and he became self-conscious and almost stopped.

But her tongue was a short tongue, and just then Eleanor Rigby started scratching at the bathroom door and Shera pounded a backhand fist against it twice, then moved her mouth from his mouth to his neck and the dog whined and pawed once more, then stopped and padded away and she—Shera, not the pooch—nibbled the skin where the edge of his jaw became his throat, then she surprised him by slurping his earlobe like it was an oyster that would not detach from its shell, and Nick reached his arms around his wife and he held her soft, pink flesh, and it felt like she was made of salt-water taffy on a hot August day, and he was dissolving into her and everything he'd worried about was dissolving too—his body, his future, his identity—and she reached a hand around behind him to the gentle arch of his lower back, and she pulled him toward her, but really, how much closer could they get?—there was no space between their skin at all, then her hand went lower, toward his tailbone, where there was a grove of still-damp hair, and oh, she loved that he was hirsute, she often told him it was a sign of strength and manliness, and she worked her fingers through the hair, tugging slightly because she knew that he liked the feeling of his hair being pulled, and…

…then she felt it.

Her eyes popped open and her head jolted up.

"What's this?" she said.

He wilted and shrivelled, like a leech in salt. "What's what?"

She pinched it, softly flicked it. "There's something on your back. Right here, just above your butt." She asked him to spin around so she could take a look, but he didn't move. He was frozen, silent.

What does one do?

What does one say?

She squeezed it. "It's stuck here. Does this hurt?" He pinched his lips and shook his head. The thing snapped off. "Oops!" she said, then brought the little mood-crusher to eye level, between them. He thought about acting surprised, but all he could do was cringe and screw his face back.

"Oh! Cute," she said. "A little mushroom. I was worried for a minute there."

She put the mushroom on the counter between her estrogen pills and Emma's acne cream and some heartburn pills for when the baby's position within Greta caused her digestive juices to climb up her throat.

Nick felt relief, like a noose around his neck had been cut. If Shera wasn't worried about it, clearly there was no reason he needed to be. He supposed mushrooms must be commonplace on men of his age, and he felt slightly embarrassed not to have known. He was overweight, over-hairy, over-fertile. And he was loved.

They laughed at his paranoia, his "little freak-out," as she called it. She made him open wide and show her the one inside his mouth that he'd decided to keep. She couldn't believe she hadn't felt it with her tongue when she was kissing him. He made a joke about her tongue being a bit on the stubby side, and she swatted him for teasing her. They talked about nurse logs and decomposing and mushroom-stuffed ravioli and dying and fairy rings and the strange miracle-bags that were men's bodies and women's bodies and finally, finally, they made love. Nick standing, Shera sitting on the counter next to the sink where she was the perfect height. They needed lube, and Nick grabbed a bottle of leave-in conditioner because it was within reach but Shera said she wasn't putting anything with a pineapple scent inside her. Greta's stretch-mark cream was right there too, and although Shera couldn't read the ingredients without her glasses, even with her arms stretched out as far as they could, she could make out the word *Organic*, and that was good enough.

They were interrupted only once when his mother banged against the door—Nick told her he was taking a dump; Shera pressed her hand against her mouth to stifle her giggles.

When they finished, they sat—naked, silent, on a pile of towels on the floor, her between his straddling legs. She leaned her back against his chest, arms around his knees. He caressed her brittle hair, which he called silver and she called grey.

"I think I lost my job this afternoon," he whispered.

"I know. I saw the email from J.J."

"Email?"

"Sorry. Your computer was open. You know how nosy I am."

"He said the world is changing and I'm not relevant."

She turned herself to face him, and put her hands on the sides of his face. "The world is the world and you are you. Everything else is a matter of opinion. Did you read the severance package they're offering? It isn't bad, but I think you should appeal. Just on principle. No need to accept their first offer. You're worth more than anyone thinks."

He hadn't considered the severance pay.

Again, a bang on the door. "Dad, Malcolm needs to use the bathroom. Hurry up!"

Malcolm? Nick mouthed to Shera. She shrugged her shoulders.

"Hi in there, Mr. Price," said a deep voice Nick had never heard before. "Nice to kind of meet you."

"Emma? What happened to lacrosse?" said Nick.

"It was cancelled. Where's Mom?"

Shera shook her head and motioned for Nick not to say anything. She quietly dug through the bathroom towels for her clothes.

More feet pounded down the hall. "Get out of my way." It was Greta. "I have to pee. Now!"

"Move it! Everybody! She has to pee! It's an emergency!" said Bradley.

"Hey, Malcolm was here first," said Emma.

"Would whoever is rattling the doorknob please stop?" said Nick.

"Who the hell's Malcolm?" said Greta.

"Oh, you can go before me," said Malcolm. "Really. I don't mind waiting."

"Thanks, bro," said Bradley. "The way the uterus rests on her bladder makes it super hard for her to maintain, like, control of her pelvic floor, you know? It's a final trimester thing."

"It's an all-the-fucking-time thing," Greta snarled.

"Oh. Here's where the party is." It was Nick's mother. "I'll go get some lemonade. It's no trouble at all."

The bathroom door opened and everyone stopped talking when Nick and Shera walked out hand in hand.

"All yours," said Nick. Bradley elbowed space for Greta.

The mushroom from the small of Nick's back stayed on the counter among the clutter for the rest of the evening and until the following Tuesday, when someone knocked it to the floor and Eleanor Rigby ate it.

Fluidity

This year: The winter morning air is nasty and bright and honest, like lights snapped on at the pub at closing time. Like consciousness after surgery. Elliot finds himself standing chest deep in the lake, among bobbing chunks of ice and snow. He gasps for breath. He doesn't remember how he came to be here. But something tells him it's where he must stay.

Last year: Elliot orders his sixth or seventh or eighth double-spiced Captain Morgan's rum and Coke at the Spread Eagle. The place is packed. Seems the whole town is there for the New Year's Eve Ball. Alone, he leans his forearm on the sticky bar and watches people. He recognizes nearly everyone. But aside from the bartender, Elliot hasn't spoken to anyone all night.

This year: His teeth are clenched so hard it feels as if they're moving up into his cheekbones. His vision is blurry. The winter water bites him, gnaws on him, like a bad dog on a table leg. His testicles, in a panic, have shrivelled and retreated into his body.

Last year: Elliot finishes the rum, chews on some ice. A woman sidles up beside him, holding a sweet vodka drink in a can. Her arms wrap around his neck. This kind of thing doesn't happen to Elliot, and he almost falls over. She smells like cigarettes and coconut shampoo; her skin is soft and warm. Says she's had her eye on him. Her eye on him? She tells him her name, but he doesn't quite hear it, and she pulls him onto the dance floor. Sara? Clara? Samantha? Are they dancing? Has he met her before? Is he imagining this? She's wearing some kind of plastic party crown with fake diamonds, rubies and emeralds. The kind a five-year-old would wear to a birthday party. She closes her eyes and sings as she dances. He suspects there's a husband or a boyfriend or an ex nearby who she's trying to make jealous.

This year: In the lake, an icy dagger twists itself into the back of Elliot's brain. This is so much worse than the dull, pounding hangover headache he knows so well. This pain stepped on his hangover and boosted itself to the top shelf.

Last year: Sara Clara Samantha readjusts the crown and yells, "You know what you should do?" Her words slide together above the music as if they're on skates. "To prove you're worthy? You should do the Polar Bear Swim tomorrow morning. They're gonna smash a hole in the lake with a backhoe!" She taps him on the nose, and says "A. Big. Cold. Dark. Fucking. Ice. Hole." One word for each tap.

He pulls back, partly from the shock of her finger on his face and partly from her suggestion.

"You think I'm kidding? You think I'm bullshitting you? I'm totally serious! Don't you know I'm a goddamn prrrrrr-rincess? I'm looking for a prrrrrrrince. Consider this your test. See if you're good enough for me."

She seems very drunk but he doesn't trust his judgment, because he is very drunk. He opens and shuts his mouth like a trout on a sandbar—out of his element and unable to think of what to say.

"Have courage. Be bold. Rise to the challenge." She runs a finger down the front of his shirt, stopping on his belt buckle and hooking her finger there. "Oh, and also? My Japanese homestay student is doing it. So there's no reason you shouldn't too."

This year: He wills his body to relax. *THREE-TWO-ONE-STOP-SHIVERING.* And it does stop, for about two seconds, then a frigid spasm reverberates from the base of his spinal cord, travels through him like a music note along a violin string, a high G-sharp perhaps, and his body begins quaking again. He is surrounded by others; men in Speedos or shorts, women in bikinis. Some have T-shirts over their bathing suits. All of them are leaping, shrieking and splashing.

Last year: "The girl, Yukiko or Yumiko, I can never remember—is that bad?—she has, like, zero body fat. She's 100 per cent lean meat and bones. Thin as a rrrrrrrrrr-rail." She grabs the roll of fat around Elliot's waist and gives it a little jostle, suggesting he has enough blubber to protect himself.

Most years he stays home on holidays. Most nights he drinks alone. He can't remember what possessed him to come out on this particular New Year's Eve.

This year: Some people dolphin-dive under the surface. Some plug their noses and drop straight down, shoot straight back up, like bowling pins that won't sink. Some barely go past their knees. Spouses and parents and lovers and first aid attendants wait with towels, bathrobes, grimaces and frowns. They are hugging themselves, as if it will help the others. Some are cheering. Some have hands over their mouths. They can't believe people would subject themselves to the frigid waters. For what?

There is hot chocolate. There is a bonfire.

And almost as quickly as they are in, the Polar Bear Swim participants are out. The caring people call the wet people crazy and wrap them up. The crazy people call the dry people chicken and snuggle near them, hopping up and down to warm up.

But Elliot stays in the lake.

The people on the shore are like royal subjects on cobblestones. Suddenly he has a memory of a crown, glittering with priceless gemstones, and he knows he is there for a higher purpose. He can't quite recall the details, but there is an invisible anchor holding him in the lake like the pull of country, state, loyalty, tradition.

The cold slaps him, over and over, harder and sharper. And yet, despite the protests of his skin, he stays. The anchor, he knows, is his own willpower.

Last year: Confetti flickers down. Streamers. The paper tube of a noisemaker smacks Elliot in the cheek. Sweat rolls down his back, stains the armpits of his Canucks T-shirt. Tequila shooters are downed. Sara Clara Samantha empties three in quick succession. "Take that, Cinderella," she snorts after slamming the last shot glass down. Music blares: Daft Punk. Bass reverberates through his sternum. Arms punch air. Breasts heave.

"Ten! Nine! Eight!"

With each number, the crowd jumps as one.

This year: Now there are only two of them in the glacial mountain lake more suitable for hockey and ice fishing and photographing than swimming. Elliot and a scrawny Japanese teenager, her thin arms crossed casually over her bikini top. She is from foreign territory, another land. She stares straight ahead, face the colour of pickled ginger. Wisps of black hair that escaped from her high ponytail have become icy white filaments at her temples.

But she isn't shaking like he is. Her lips are dry and colourless and there is a layer of frosty crystals on her eyelashes, but otherwise she doesn't even look cold. She could be waiting for a bus or listening for a bird to sing. Steam is spiralling off her head. She might even be smiling.

Last year: "Seven! Six! Five!" He steps on someone's foot and is called a fuck-tard. The air swings with sweat, hair, hands, beer bottles, champagne glasses, strings of plastic pearls, curls of coloured paper, open mouths. A drink drops. Ice cubes and shards of glass scatter and bounce and nobody cares. Sara Clara Samantha's crown stays on her head, but her blouse slips off her shoulder. Elliot notices the lime-green bra strap. She should be more modest, he thinks. He moves forward, pinches the fabric of her blouse and pulls it back onto her shoulder. This is bold for Elliot, but there's so much noise and confusion he doesn't feel quite like himself. The blouse falls down her shoulder again and this time he stares, as if in a trance. Lime green doesn't seem like a suitable colour for a princess's bra. But what would he know about princesses? Or women? Or bras? Or green?

This year: Every nerve, every fibre, every cell tells him to leave the lake, but he is no longer loyal to his own body's wishes. The crowd is cheering. Look how boisterous they are! And the girl—they cheer for her too. She's a tough little motherfucker, and the whole town loves the thrill of competition. Who has the greatest willpower? Perhaps they've never seen two people with such self-control. He has cast a spell over his body.

His heart feels like it might try and make a run for shore on its own, but he ignores the impulse. He doesn't think he's ever, in his entire life, overridden a physical urge through sheer determination. It feels incredible, this power. It's a higher state of being.

The black-haired girl looks at Elliot and nods her head toward the shore. She's telling him to go. *Go in?* She wants him to give up! Is she out of her mind? She doesn't know what it's like to be him. To never face a new challenge. To never be watched. Adored. Respected.

It's this bone-cracking cold, this pain, the intensity of the crowd, this bright, perfect, first morning of the year; he's never felt so alive. He knows he can conquer this lake and this icy young rival and all his own weaknesses. He knows he can conquer his own body's superficial needs and transcend his own skin. He is stronger than his own survival instinct. He has passed a test.

Elliot presses his lips together, flares his nostrils, tightens his arms around his chest and looks away from the girl. He imagines trumpets blasting. For the first time ever, he feels like his mind is the king of his physical self.

Go back in? he thinks. *Ha! Fat chance, bitch.*

Last year: "Four! Three! Two!" It's so loud he can't hear anything, just a roar like an avalanche inside his skull. The room spins. He reaches for the princess's hand, but she isn't there. Was she ever there at all? Elliot can't be sure. The walls undulate like the surface of cold water on a windy day.

This year: "Get out of the lake, asshole!" yells someone from shore. "Who *is* that guy? He's insane!" "Look at the girl. Whose kid is she? She can't be more than fourteen years old." "Hey, big shot, what are you trying to prove? Beating a kid?" Others are more supportive. "Ice! Man! Ice! Man! Ice Man!" and "Can't be all that cold," and "Dude, you don't look too good."

The girl reaches her hand toward him and he suddenly knows how she wants this to end. She wants them to emerge from the water *together*, heroes of two nations, arms in the air, sharing the victory. She's offering a truce.

He pictures the scene that lies ahead: women swarming him with bathrobes and warm drinks. Men patting him on the back and ruffling his hair. They will say that he has shown rare strength, that in his courage to disregard his body's physical needs, he has inspired them all. He'll be a rock star, that's what he'll be. He will tell the onlookers that enduring hardships is simply mind over matter. That true power and strength comes from within, and that extremes of hot and cold, like the ecstasy of love and the agony of loss, are good for the heart. Then, from the back of the crowd, he will see a beautiful, familiar face beaming at him. His dream woman. His queen.

But not just yet. There is a decision to be made. Does he take the girl's hand and share the victory? Or does he try to outlast her and claim his throne as the bravest person in town?

As he weighs both options everything turns grey and grimy, the colour of a dance floor, the colour of mould. There is a hard flutter in his chest. His heart is like a dove stuck in a mailbox. He hears a gasp and a crack and the surface of the water becomes his surface.

Last year: His vision is blurry, but the last thing he registers before vomiting all over the dance floor at the Spread Eagle is the woman of royal ancestry kissing a short man in a baseball cap that says *Keiwit Construction*. A curly streamer hangs from her crown like a long ringlet and Elliot knows she will never warm his bed.

"One! Hap..."

This year: The woman on the couch in the living room of a townhouse across the train tracks near the south end of the lake can't quite recall how many men she ended up making out with the night before. She's still wearing her party clothes, wrinkled and itchy, and full makeup. She's been there since crawling out of a taxi a few hours before the dawn of the new year broke. There's a radio blaring from down the hall. Must be coming from that homestay girl's alarm clock. *What did she have to get up early for, today of all days?* thinks the woman. *The girl can't press "snooze"? She can't press "off"? What's she doing now?*

She doesn't like listening to the blathering DJs, but she doesn't have the energy to get up and walk down into the spare bedroom the Japanese kid is using and turn the radio off. The DJs joke about breaking their own New Year's resolutions, about the after-effects of last night's parties, about predictions for the upcoming twelve months, then play "Hair of the Dog" by Nazareth. There's an ad for brunch at the Spread Eagle for seven dollars and ninety-nine cents including coffee. Eggs, bacon, hash browns and orange juice. The thought of food makes her feel nauseous. She runs her thumb along the rubies and emerald and diamonds on the tiara she bought at Dollarama the day before and vows never to drink again.

Last year: "...py New Year!"

This year: At the lakeshore, the ambulance's double back doors slam shut and Yumiko watches the emergency vehicle pull out of the parking lot. She cinches her scarf tightly around her neck and stands with the quiet crowd. Sirens have a different cadence in Osaka, but they both inspire the same feeling: *Thank God it's not me in there.*

She doesn't quite know what to do next.

It seems no one does.

There is chatter, but people speak so quickly here, and she only catches snippets. The man from the lake might die; he might already be dead. She doesn't know who to ask or how to phrase it. If he is dead, he's the first dead person she's ever seen. If he's not, it's the first life she's ever saved. In any case, he's the hairiest person she's ever seen. His skin was covered in what looked to her like a coat of fur. Like a bear. She is surprised this hair sweater did not better protect him from the cold.

She will never forget the seconds before the man collapsed. His eyes rolled up toward the heavens, his mouth curled into a gentle smile like the arc of a canoe, a shallow dish, and his bluish lips parted as if he were about to speak. And as he slowly tipped backwards, he put his hand—the one that wasn't grasping hers—upon his heart. Not like he was having a heart attack but like he was swearing allegiance to something very powerful.

On the long walk back to her homestay she thinks of her nearly hairless father. Legs, chest, face and head, completely smooth. He hadn't supported his daughter's trip to Canada alone; didn't understand why she'd want to go to a country that really doesn't have much of anything besides lakes and trees and open spaces. He thought the people in Canada did not have modesty. Or loyalty. Or discipline. That they were perhaps just a little too outrageous.

Happy?

For the first decade of their marriage Babs Johnson had been fairly game, sexually speaking. Twice, sometimes three times a week, for approximately fifteen minutes, she and Phil would explore each other the way men and women have throughout history. "Shall we intertwine?" was his usual come-on, and it usually worked. Phil occasionally brought home something in a plain brown paper bag from the Naughty Shop, just for "extra kicks." But despite reading the instructions carefully, they never could quite figure out how to use it, insert it or turn it on and the thingamabob usually wound up at the back of her nightstand drawer after one or two awkward tries. "Never mind," Phil would say. "We don't need gadgets. We have each other." And he meant it. He was usually satisfied and she was usually comforted.

In the second decade of their marriage, the Johnsons' lovemaking decreased in frequency, duration and, at least for Babs, quality. But Phil was a simple man, and they were polite to each other. He would wait until she was finished the chapter of whatever self-help book she was reading, then gently slide her glasses off her face, insert her bookmark, lean across and click off the light on her side, and slide her nightie up over her head. Seven to ten minutes later they'd both put in their dental apparatuses and roll apart. After he'd twitched a few times, she'd turn her light back on and read some more. Or just look out the skylight over their bed to the silent stars above and wonder why she bothered, what all the fuss was about.

By their third decade of marriage, sex simply didn't seem worth the effort. Like cooking risotto, she saw it as a messy nuisance with results that didn't justify all that stirring. She had no urge to leave her husband—they were compatible in so many other ways—but Babs yearned for a life of celibacy and contemplation. Life in the garden. Quiet meditation. Peace. Spirituality that wasn't connected to the carnal.

Not Phil. "Hubba hubba," he'd say whenever he accidentally-on-purpose walked into the bathroom while she was in the tub. "What a goddess you are." His libido was as strong as ever, and it was Babs he wanted.

She finally put her foot down, albeit gently. "Can't we just cuddle?" she'd say. "Getting it on just doesn't interest me anymore."

He reminded her that he was a hot-blooded man with certain needs and desires. She watered the miniature rubber fig tree on the kitchen windowsill and let out a sigh as the moisture seeped into the soil.

"Look, if you want it that badly go have an affair. Honestly. It wouldn't bother me one bit. I want you to be happy. I just don't want to be responsible for your happiness anymore." She rattled off the names of several neighbourhood women she figured would be more than willing.

Phil couldn't imagine being with anyone else. Even when given permission—even when *encouraged*—he would not cheat on his wife of thirty-two and a half years.

"If I can't have you, I'd just as soon my 'love muscle' shrivelled up and popped right off my body," he said. Oh, the curse of a faithful man!

Babs, desperate to break the cycle of rejection, frustration, guilt and reluctant participation, knew she had to take action. So on a breezy Thursday morning in May, when she was in the garage looking for the spade and spotted a tube of Canadian Tire Silicone Plus Latex Caulking and a caulking gun on a shelf behind some cans of paint, an idea dawned on her. Maybe it was the shape of the tube, not unlike one of the Naughty Shop items Phil had once brought home, or maybe it was the word *caulk*. She picked it up. *Indoor/Outdoor! Highly Durable! Mildew Resistant! 35-Year Guarantee!* announced the words up the side of the cylinder. *Recommended by Experts for Impenetrable Sealing Around Plumbing Fixtures!*

Babs knew exactly what to do. Even though Phil wouldn't be home until six and the neighbourhood women who went for their power walks in duos and trios never stopped by, she needed absolute privacy. She locked the garage door, then she removed the plastic cap, snipped the narrow end of the stiff blue-and-white cardboard tube with scissors (as per the instructions), placed it into the holder (for ease of application), lifted her skirt, pulled her underpants down to her ankles, wrapped her hair into a quick ponytail, stood with her legs apart and knees bent like she was about to insert a gigantic tampon, and squirted the cool white goop generously along the inside of each of her labia.

The product was thick and smooth, like the fabric paint she'd once used to decorate her Keds. It smelled like vinegar and bananas. She wondered briefly whether she should have put on a face mask but figured there would have been some kind of warning if the product or its fumes were toxic.

When there was a thick layer of sealant, she held her breath and pinched her outer lips together. She counted to sixty, and even though the instructions said it would be up to twelve hours before the sealant was completely cured, she knew the silicone had begun to set. Her sex was a lily at night, folding in on itself. By the time she exhaled and released her fingers, it was curtains closed on vagina-town. Lights out. Door latched. Game over. Out of commission. She used a moist towelette to wipe a few white blobs off the inside of her thigh and one off the garage floor, leaned against a work bench, waited another three minutes and pulled her panties up.

"It's my love handles, isn't it?" said Phil when he reached under her nightie and felt the impenetrable rubbery seam. As a carpenter, he recognized the smell and feel of the tacky substance right away. He knew she'd caulked herself. "When it comes right down to it, I don't turn you on anymore because I'm too fat. Right? Am I right?"

She held his big pyramid-shaped face in her hands and kissed him and told him not to be ridiculous. That he was still as handsome as ever, and she still loved him. It wasn't him, she said. It was her. She just felt it was time to move into a less physical relationship. Something more spiritual, based on quiet companionship. Being sealed would eliminate the arguments. Remove the source of his temptation.

Babs was perspiring. There was an unusual sheen on her back, her forehead and the palms of her hands.

"Quiet companionship?" said Phil. "You can get that from a plant!"

He moped for a bit, then suggested they try anal. He said that she might really like it. "I know it's a little weird, but I promise to be gentle."

She felt obliged to give it a whirl, but it was terrible and she couldn't fake that it wasn't, so the next morning she poked a tube of Gorilla Glue into her anus and squirted the contents inside. It was cold at first, but once it dried it felt quite natural. A relief, really. And since she'd lost her appetite for food since the caulking, her digestive system had pretty much called it quits.

"I knew it," said Phil, when he saw the empty glue tube beside the bathroom sink. "You haven't been attracted to me since my hairline started receding. I'm just a fat, balding old man. Oh God, is there someone else?"

His insecurities drove her nuts. Why was it so hard for him to understand? Babs was happiest soaking in the tub, sitting on a lawn chair in the sunshine, feeling around for potatoes in the soil out back. At night she preferred to watch the moon and breathe the fresh, cool air. She was okay being touched. A back rub, sure. A little foot massage, or a cuddle, nice. She'd simply decided to close her borders to foreign invasion. Wasn't a woman free to maintain her entrances? To control access?

"You need to stop taking things personally," said Babs. "Besides, look at Matthew McConaughey. He has a receding hairline, big time! And he's super hot. I love you, but I need to be in control of my own body. I need my spaces to be *my* spaces." It was time for the simplicity of witnessing the changing seasons. Of being a part of the wider world.

"Really?" said Phil, perking up. "Do you really think I look like Matthew McConaughey?" Then he told her he'd always enjoyed their anniversary and birthday oral sex, and that he wouldn't mind if she wanted to picture someone else while she was at it.

Afterwards, Babs said, "No offence, but..." and sealed off her mouth with duct tape.

"I don't blame you," he said. "It's probably because I can't properly provide for us financially. We thought we'd be retired by now. Travelling the world. Debt free."

That evening, Babs put her head on his shoulder and they watched a TED Talk about photosynthesis. Glucose in, oxygen out. So pure. So beautiful. She touched his thigh through his sweats while they watched, moving her fingers gently, the way you'd scratch an old dog's head.

Phil misunderstood her intentions. When the show was over he told her he'd always fantasized about her nose and asked if he could stick his pinky finger up inside.

Babs sewed her nostrils closed with fishing twine.

"We could try in your ear? Do it in the cochlea?"

She crossed her arms and sighed. The exhale came through her pores. He began telling her about a recent episode of *Quirks and Quarks* that confirmed the relationship between the condition of vasocongestion—otherwise known as blue balls—and penile atrophy. But she filled her ears with pottery clay and went to bed, not hearing the end of the story.

The clay hardened by morning. There was no way anything or anyone was getting in or out of there.

"My body, my rules," Babs mumbled through the duct tape. "Full self-sufficiency." She knew Phil couldn't actually hear her. That was okay. She gazed out the window at the arbutus tree across the street, whose smooth, curved limbs reminded her of a dancer.

"Maybe watching a little porn together would help?" said Phil. "Nothing too kinky, mind you. Just mainstream stuff. A bit of girl on girl? To get you back in the mood?"

Babs couldn't hear him but could read his lips. She understood every word. As he searched "TubeKitty" on his laptop, she pulled her top and bottom eyelids out by the lashes and pinched them together with wooden clothespins.

It was complete. She was a self-contained unit. She felt like an astronaut. Like a seed in a pod. She lay on the couch under the window, in a patch of sunshine. She sensed heavy footsteps crossing the room.

For a moment, she was afraid he'd go to the hall closet, get the duffle bag and pack his things. There was a catch in her throat. What if he left? What had she been thinking? A drip of snot escaped through a gap in the fishing twine. She tried to sniff it back. She knew he loved her, but maybe this was pushing it too far.

The footsteps came closer. Instead of going to the closet, Phil slid his arms underneath Babs and lifted her up. He was a sweaty hammock, warm and thick, and she was a house without windows or doors. She felt a kiss on her forehead, his breath close to her face. There was a tiny splash. Then another one. Were those his teardrops?

Phil cradled Babs and she felt as if she were three years old, being carried from the car seat to bed after a long road trip. She was filled with a sweet mixture of dizziness and helplessness. There was a change in the air pressure and temperature. She felt a light breeze on her skin. He'd opened the back door. Her foot smacked something—the side of the house?—and the warm afternoon sun enveloped her like water in a bathtub.

They bumped down the steps off the deck. Gently, he set her on the grass. It felt cool and ticklish on her bare feet. She held his arm at the elbow and walked tentatively forward, hunched over like a blind woman, step by step, until the grass ended and soft garden soil welcomed her. She curled her toes, gripping and ungripping the squishy earth like a cat making itself comfortable on a pillow. She felt as if she'd finally landed on firm ground. As she wiggled her feet and toes around, she sank slowly down, down into the soil.

Eventually the earth encompassed her ankles. Then her knees. Hips. At about belly button level she stopped sinking. She was rooted. Phil knelt beside her, holding her hand in quiet companionship. Babs could feel her heart rate slow, her breath deepen. She had the sense that her blood was getting thicker. The hush felt like home. The warm May sun shone upon her face and it was peaceful until Phil, being Phil, guided her hand gently between his legs.

Where were his pants?

Babs was yanked from her reverie. Some things never changed. However, she was feeling relaxed and generous. What was the harm? She wrapped her fingers around his penis, for old times' sake.

To her amazement, with the first tug of her wrist, his "love muscle" popped clean off in her hand. The entire shaft. She held it, horrified and confused, then flipped it over a few times and rolled it between her palms, like a drunk vegan on a dare with some bratwurst. She brought it to her face and dragged it along her cheek, remembering. It was soft and cool. A bit sticky. It might have had a smell; needless to say, she couldn't detect one. She placed it tenderly on the ground beside her and reached for her husband, but he was no longer there.

Obviously, the penisectomy hurt Phil like a son-of-a-bitch, although the science show had been right and some atrophy had already occurred. He staggered to the perimeter of the garden, grabbed handfuls of plantain leaves ("nature's healing weed") and pressed them between his legs to stem the bleeding and numb the area. But what really put him over the edge was the sight of a dachshund that had trotted playfully into the yard when he heard Phil's cry of anguish, scooped the detached member out of the mud and shook it like it was some kind of stuffed chew toy.

Phil vomited all over the deck. After his final heave, he looked up and wiped his mouth on his sleeve. The dog was gone. Knick knack paddywhack, indeed. "Happy?" he said to Babs. He didn't intend to sound sarcastic, and was relieved that she could not hear him. He suspected that finally, she was. He wished he could say the same for himself.

In the house, he pulled away the plantain, packed the vacant space where his organ had been with a mixture of local organic honey and Polysporin, bandaged the wound and popped four extra-strength Tylenol. Then he went back outside, got the hose from the shed and set the sprinkler on low in the garden. There was a little rainbow in the arc of droplets. Babs seemed to bask in the water and mist. Even though she was half-buried in the earth and void of all senses and orifices, she was still beautiful, in an eerily meditative way. Like a Stephen King version of a Buddha statue.

Days went by, and May turned to June. Babs had no demands, made no complaints, expressed no desires. Phil's crotch healed nicely, but he was envious of his wife. She was completely self-sufficient. She was thriving. He pulled the weeds that grew near her, out of respect. He sprinkled the area with organic fertilizer, out of love. He put up a little fence to keep critters away, out of protectiveness. Within a few weeks, her skin became crusty and grey. Her torso shrank until it was no bigger than a stick. Tiny shoots appeared on her head and neck. Eventually the duct tape peeled off and blew away. The unfired pottery clay became mushy from all the watering and dribbled out. Although the silicone caulking was a man-made polymer that was not biodegradable, the fishing twine did break down and the wooden clothespins rotted, warped and slid off.

Bab's skin had turned to thin, papery bark.

By midsummer, she was a rose bush.

Neighbourhood women in tank tops and Lululemon pants brought casseroles by for Phil. Banana bread. They told him they'd always thought Babs had been a very lucky woman. They couldn't believe she'd run off, just like that. "The grass is always greener on the other side of the fence," they'd recite. "She's crazy to leave a catch like you." They told him that their husbands were workaholics who didn't understand them. They told him that they knew a little bit about loneliness themselves. They asked him if he was ticklish.

The more he ignored their flirtations, the more blatant they became.

Kirsten drew her finger across her bottom lip and told him he had the body of a long-distance runner.

Dagmar put a hand on his knee, said he reminded her of Richard Branson and suggested they go out dancing one night.

Terri-Jane said she wanted to fuck his brains out.

You couldn't blame the women for being attracted to him. There's a certain confidence exuded by a humble man who seems ambivalent toward sex, a man who could take it or leave it.

"He just seems so *spiritual*," said Lynette, who said she didn't care whether he was well-hung or not. "I bet he's into doing it all Kama Sutra, tantric-style."

They told him that no, of course they didn't think it was weird, the amount of time he stood out there in his back garden, barefoot in the soil, with his arms in the air like some kind of scarecrow, next to that rose bush. Maybe they were lying. Maybe they did think it was weird, but just liked the idea of an eccentric single man who still wore his wedding ring—the strong, silent, dedicated, earthy type—and they were just trying not to hurt his feelings.

It's true that his body had become long and lithe, his skin a smooth amber hue. However, he would not have described himself as having the limbs of a dancer. When he looked in the mirror, he saw more of an Ichabod Crane type—the cartoon version. But the more time he spent with his bare feet planted in the soil in the back garden and his face to the sun, the more he understood the allure of photosynthesis. Of warmth, and sunshine, and quiet companionship.

The neighbourhood women did not have long attention spans. When Phil didn't answer the door or take their calls for almost a week, they gave up on him. "I figure he's gay," said Marie-Helene. "Maybe that's why she left him. You wouldn't believe the number of guys who retire and then come out of the closet."

"Or he's just plain off his rocker," said Tallulah. None of the women could believe he had refused all their offers. They'd literally *thrown* themselves at him.

Trinh was more compassionate. "I think he's in a state of depression. No kids, that deranged wife of his leaving him. It's hard on men to be alone. Mental illness can leave a guy limp as a wet noodle. And if he was taking meds..."

No one noticed the new arbutus tree, with its muscular, curving limbs, that had taken root in the Johnsons' garden.

Or the way its branches intertwined with those of the bush beside it, like fingers through hair. Or how tiny pink flowers opened shamelessly toward the smooth, bright green tree trunk with its peeling, blood-red bark, all those little stamens poking up at the leaves, like tongues, to lick.

Acknowledgements

I am fortunate to be surrounded by family, dear friends and a community of artists, children, seekers and dreamers who motivate me every day.

Giving birth to a short story collection is a risky endeavour. Now that this book has grown up and moved out, I'd like to back-page-hug the many people who provided support, guidance and inspiration during its creation.

Special thanks to the members of the Vicious Circle Writers Group: Stella Harvey Leventoyannis, Rebecca Wood Barrett, Sue Oakey, Libby McKeever, Mary MacDonald and Sara Leach. Within this gathering of talons, feathers and beaks there is much love. My parents, John and Leslie Stoddart, were first readers of many of these stories. Their wisdom and feedback are immeasurable. I am also extremely grateful for the mentorship, direction and inspiration of Susan Juby and Eileen Cook.

Thank you to Anna Comfort O'Keeffe for her faith in this book, and to Silas White, Emma Skagen, Brianna Cerkiewicz, Nicola Goshulak and the whole Douglas & McIntyre team for their dedication to the written word in Canada.

To Brandon Barrett: thanks for all the deadlines. And to Dan Ellis of Armchair Books: you rock!

A huge shout-out to Jen Sookfong Lee and my cohort at the Simon Fraser University Writer's Studio. Over the years, I have also benefited greatly from immersion in the Whistler

Writers Festival, the Whistler Writer in Residence program and the Writers Adventure Camp.

Josh, Megan, Scott and Kirsten: I'm so lucky to have a gaggle of wonderful siblings.

Emma Wardrop: this woman is the consummate teacher. I admire her strength and resilience. The world is a better place because of her.

Andrea Purton is a philosopher banjo queen who helps me hear what's under the melody.

I have learned about discipline, focus and the power of quiet kindness from Yuko Iwanaga.

I am grateful to John Dippong and his family for showing me a better way to make potatoes.

Janet Corvino helps me see clearly.

Tammy McIvor always asks the right questions.

Jonathon Fenton taught me the art of embellishment and humility in storytelling. No one can make me laugh like Jonny and Laura.

Thank you to Rubeena Sandhu, Gabriel Alden Hull and both Waldorf communities in Whistler and Squamish for flexibility and support as I strive for a journey of balance.

My friends in the Sea to Sky Orchestra, in Right Turn Clyde and in the bluegrass/old time music community are precious to me. These connections feed my soul, ignite my curiosity and stoke my imagination.

Jack and Lilah deserve buckets of credit for putting up with all the ideas I bounce off them. They are two of the most amazing people I've ever had the pleasure of getting to know.

And thank you to Bob, whose kindness, support and patience does not waver.

During the writing of this book, I lost a beloved cat and a dog. April and Bumble's spirits (and perhaps a bit of their fur) live within these pages.

This book would not have been possible without generous

financial assistance from the Canada Council for the Arts.

Original versions of several stories appeared in the following publications: “Happy?” in *Grain,* “The Pull of Old Rat Creek”” in *CVC Short Fiction Anthology Book Seven* from Exile Editions, “The Maternal Instinct of Witches,” “Mary Wonderful’s New Grimoire,” “Fluidity” and “What the Cat Coughed Up” in *Pique Newsmagazine.*